WARRIOR KING

SUE PURKISS is the author of several novels for young readers, including *Spook School*, *Changing Brooms*, *Spooks Away* and *The Willow Man*. She lives in Cheddar, Somerset.

Of *Warrior King*, Sue says, "A few years ago, I was writing a story which had a reference to King Alfred and how he burnt the cakes he was supposed to be looking after because he was so busy planning how to defeat the Vikings.

"The more I read, the more fascinated I became. Here was a Dark Age ruler who was not only a great warrior but also a scholar, a man who cared about learning. The only English monarch to be known as "the Great", he was a king who left his country far stronger and a better place to live in than when he came to the throne. He was a remarkably interesting man.

"Yet today, while everyone knows all about the legendary King Arthur, few people know much about the very real King Alfred.

"I realized that Athelney, where Alfred proved to be such a useless cook, is only about fifteen miles from where I live. I decided to go there, expecting to find lots of information about him, a shop called Alfred's Cakes, a café called Burnt Offerings – that kind of thing.

"There was nothing like that. There was a low green hill with a stumpy stone monument, and apart from that, just a magical landscape, with rows of willows, water birds calling above stretches of floodwater and Glastonbury Tor in the distance.

"As I leaned on a gate looking at the hill – at Alfred's Athelney – an old man came up to me. 'Ah,' he said – and I swear this is absolutely true – 'you'll be looking for Alfred.'

"And that's what I've been doing ever since, and what this book is about. Looking for Alfred."

WARRIOR
KING

SUE PURKISS

**WALKER
BOOKS**

First published 2008 by Walker Books Ltd
87 Vauxhall Walk, London SE11 5HJ

2 4 6 8 10 9 7 5 3 1

Text © 2008 Sue Purkiss
Cover illustration © 2008 Steve Rawlings

The right of Sue Purkiss to be identified as author of this work
has been asserted by her in accordance with the Copyright, Designs
and Patents Act 1988.

This book has been typeset in Weiss and Francesca

Printed in Great Britain by CPI Bookmarque, Croydon, CR0 4TD

British Library Cataloguing in Publication Data:
a catalogue record for this book is available
from the British Library

ISBN 978-1-4063-0844-0

www.walkerbooks.co.uk

Contents

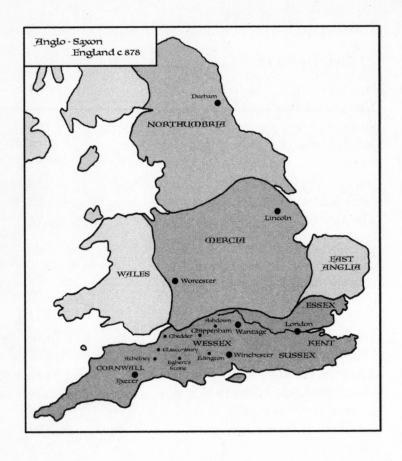

IN THE NINTH CENTURY, ENGLAND WASN'T ONE COUNTRY DIVIDED INTO COUNTIES, AS IT IS TODAY; IT CONSISTED OF SEVERAL DIFFERENT KINGDOMS. THIS MAP SHOWS APPROXIMATELY WHERE THE BOUNDARIES WERE.

In memory of Bill Purkiss, and for Bron

PROLOGUE

"From the fury of the Northmen, O Lord, deliver us!"
(Ninth-century prayer)

At the beginning of the ninth century, England didn't exist as it is now. It was divided up into a number of separate kingdoms: Northumbria in the north, Mercia in the midlands, East Anglia in the east, Kent in the south-east, and Wessex in the south-west.

There were disputes sometimes between the kingdoms but, mostly, life was good. There was plenty of rich farmland, so there was enough to eat. Traders travelled throughout the world, bringing back exotic goods to sell in the markets and stories of the sights they had seen. The life of the soul was nurtured by great monasteries, founded by charismatic holy men like Cuthbert and Aidan.

But a dark shadow was reaching out from Scandinavia. The Vikings were growing restless. They had ships, sleek and swift, and they used the sea as a road to take them wherever they wanted to go. Sometimes they went as traders. More often, it was as pirates.

One of their first targets in Britain was Lindisfarne, a monastery famous throughout Europe for its devotion and learning. It was an easy target because it was on an island, just off the Northumbrian coast. The Viking dragon ships swept across the North Sea, disgorging their savage crews to steal what was useful and set fire to everything else. They seized the younger monks for slaves and casually slaughtered the old and the weak.

And this was to be the pattern. Islands were easy, but nowhere was safe. The great rivers of Europe carried them right into the heart of the continent, so that, in time, they would ransack Paris and even threaten Rome, the very centre of the Christian world.

They were as cruel as a winter blizzard and as impossible to resist. But at least, like a storm, they passed – until 851.

In that year, a Viking force spent the whole winter on the Isle of Thanet, just off the coast of Kent. Were they growing tired of wandering? Did they mean to settle, to take land as well as riches?

One hundred and fifty miles to the west was the court of King Aethelwulf of Wessex. The king's fifth and youngest son, Alfred, was one day to become the last great hope of the English-speaking peoples in their battle to survive the Viking onslaught.

But for the moment, he knew nothing of this. He was just a small boy, to whom something terrible was happening.

ALFRED'S STORY

First Loss: 851

A LFRED COULDN'T FIND HIS MOTHER. He'd looked in all the usual places, but she wasn't in any of them. The last time he'd seen her, she was wearing a blue dress, the same blue as the sky. The stuff the dress was made of had been soft against his face, and she'd stroked his hair as if she was stroking a bird's wing. Her other hand had rested on her tummy, which was very big, and she'd said she was sorry, but she was really tired and he must go and play.

There had been something funny in her voice, something that made him feel very frightened, and he hadn't wanted to leave her, but Hylda had made him go and told him he must be a good boy and not be a worry or the Vikings would get him. People were always talking about the Vikings. Alfred was scared of the Vikings, but just at the moment he was much more scared about his mother, and so when Hylda helped his mother into the bedroom she shared with the king, his father, he crept back and sat quietly outside the door with his knees drawn up to his chin and his thumb in his mouth. Usually if he sucked his thumb so hard that it hurt, he could go into a sort of daydream and then he wouldn't have to think about anything else.

But now there were horrible noises coming from inside the room, screams and groans, and in the end it was more frightening to stay than to go, so he fled to look for Redi, his favourite brother. But he couldn't find Redi, so he went and hid under the table in the kitchen. It felt nice and safe there.

Much later, when Hylda found him, she pulled him out and scolded him and gave him something to eat. But when Alfred asked where his mother was, Hylda just looked at him and her face went all red and crumpled and she made a funny noise and then she scurried away. So Alfred decided he would set off by himself to find his mother.

Her favourite place was the room where she often sat and sewed with the other ladies of the court. They talked and laughed as they worked, and it was usually a happy place. He tried there first.

But she wasn't there. No one was.

Then he went into the courtyard that led from the sewing room. It had a sunny garden where herbs and flowers grew, and when her skirt brushed against them it would make the air smell sweet.

She wasn't there either.

Perhaps she was with his father, the king, in the great hall. He didn't usually like to go in there by himself, but he really did need to find her.

Usually in the hall there were men's loud voices and laughter, but today everyone was very quiet. He caught a glimpse of his father in his big chair. The king was sitting still, and his eyes were closed. But he didn't look comfortably asleep – his face was creased, as if something was hurting him.

Alfred backed out. He knew the next place he should try was the room his mother had gone into with Hylda, but he couldn't go back there. It was a room full of shadows and strange noises, and he was afraid of what he would find.

Then he saw Baldu, the biggest of his three brothers. They were called Aethelbald, Aethelbert and Aethelred. His sister, Aethelswith, was grown-up and lived in Mercia, because she was married to King Burgred. There had been another brother, Aethelstan, the oldest, but he'd been killed in battle against the Vikings the year before. His brothers were all much older than he was. Aethelred – Redi – was the closest, and even he was much, much bigger than Alfred. They all had "Aethel" at the front of their name, and it meant "prince". All except him, as Baldu liked to point out.

"And why?" Baldu would taunt him. "Because you're just a silly little baby, that's why."

Alfred didn't like Baldu. He was mean and he liked to

hurt people. Once he'd twisted Alfred's ear really hard, which had surprised Alfred; up till then no one had hurt him on purpose. But Baldu said he hadn't done anything, and Alfred was just a spoiled little brat who wanted everyone to make a fuss of him. So Baldu was a liar as well.

But today he was the one who was crying. Alfred asked if he'd seen their mother, and Baldu glared at him, his eyes red-rimmed and ugly.

"Don't you know, you stupid little boy? She's dead! She's gone and she's never coming back and you'll never see her again. And neither will I!" And then he pushed roughly past Alfred, wiping his face on his sleeve. Alfred stood there all alone and tried to understand it. He felt very frightened and had no idea what he should do next. All he really wanted was his mother, but she wasn't there and he felt very, very sad, so he lifted his head and in his pain he howled like a wolf.

At least he thought he did, but really it couldn't have been all that loud, because no one heard him and no one came. He curled up very small, and wondered if it might possibly not be true, if perhaps Baldu might be lying again. But in his heart, he knew that it was. The words echoed in his head. His mother was gone, and he would never, ever see her again.

News of a Journey: 855

A LFRED LASHED OUT furiously at Redi with his wooden
sword. That last blow had really hurt – and the one
before, and the one before that. He was determined to
get his own back. He gritted his teeth and scowled
fiercely. Yet again, his sword hit thin air. Redi wasn't
where he had been a second before. Nor was his sword –
all of a sudden it was under Alfred's chin.

He pushed it aside crossly. "It's no use – I'll never be as
good as you!"

Redi burst out laughing. "Yes you will. In fact, when
you've grown – just a bit more! – you'll probably be better." And he flopped down with his back against a tree
and closed his eyes lazily. The sun was shining down
through the leaves, and a spring breeze stirred them and
set them dancing.

It was four years since their mother had died, and
though Alfred had grown a good deal, Redi was still
much older and taller.

Alfred watched his brother, puzzled. Redi was definitely his favourite brother and the one he was closest to, but sometimes Alfred just didn't understand him.

"Why?" he asked bluntly. "Why do you think I'll be better than you?"

"Because you care about winning much more than I do," said Redi simply.

Alfred turned this idea over in his mind, looking at it from all angles. He wasn't absolutely sure he liked the sound of it. Baldu liked to win, and he would much rather be like Redi than Baldu. On the other hand...

"But when you're fighting," he said slowly, "surely you want to win? Else what's the point?"

"Yes, of course, if you have to fight. But other things matter more than fighting, don't they? I'm just more interested in them, that's all. And don't ask me what they are, because you won't understand, not yet. Anyway, look," he said, jumping up. "The reason you keep losing is that you aren't holding your sword properly. You must hold it firmly, as if it's part of your arm – see, put your fingers like this."

Alfred watched closely, and tried again. He swirled the sword about experimentally, and smiled in delight.

"Yes!" he said. "You're right, that works much better!"

"Dear, oh, dear, you'll have my head off!" said an aggrieved voice. It was Hylda. "Put that thing down," she said, straightening her head cloth crossly, "and come along with me. Your father wishes to see you straight away."

Alfred stared at her blankly. "Me? Are you sure he didn't say Aethelred?" He saw his father all the time, of course, just in passing, and often his father gave him a kindly but slightly puzzled smile, as if he wasn't quite sure who he was – but he wasn't usually summoned to the king's presence like this.

"I know what I heard, and what I heard was Alfred," said Hylda briskly. "Now come along, let's have a look at you – a fine mess you are! Your tunic's all covered with twigs and bits of this and that – whatever will your father think of me?"

Alfred submitted patiently, wondering what it could be about. Perhaps Wulfric had been telling tales. Wulf looked after the pigs, and he was Alfred's friend. The big sow had had piglets and, earlier on, Alfred had let them out. They'd run all over the place, with Wulf scurrying after first one, then another. But he wouldn't have told, would he? After all, in the end Alfred had helped him and they'd got them all back.

Maybe Wulf's father had found out? Oh, well. Whatever it was, he'd better get it over with. Alfred trailed after Hylda into the great hall.

His father, King Aethelwulf, was talking to a tall man Alfred had never seen before. There were creases round the man's blue eyes, as if he was used to gazing into the distance, and his skin was as brown as a cobnut. Aethelwulf's face was lined too, but the lines were in different places; deep furrows marked his forehead and travelled from his nose to either side of his mouth. His hair shone white in a stray shaft of sunlight. Beside the other man, who stood tall and straight, Alfred's father looked stooped and weary, and Alfred felt a shock of surprise. Why, he looked old! But then the king looked at Alfred and a smile lit up his face, and with relief Alfred saw that he was once again his father and the king, the one whose strength and wisdom sheltered them all.

"Alfred," said the king, "this is Cerdic. He's the captain of a ship, and he's going to take us on a journey."

Alfred stared from one to the other, thunderstruck. "Across the sea?" he gasped.

The king smiled again. "Well, yes. I don't think it would be much good to ask a sea captain to take us on a journey by land – do you?" He turned to Cerdic. "Go and make ready. We'll follow you within the week."

Cerdic bowed, and said, "You'll never travel on a keener ship than the *Raven*, my lord, I can promise you that!" Then, with a grin at Alfred, he was gone, leaving behind just a very faint tang of salt.

Alfred turned eagerly to his father, the words now tumbling over each other. "But where, sir? And why – I mean, why me? And—"

The king held up his hands, and his laughter rang out. "Peace, Alfred! One question at a time! As for where we're going, that's easy. We're going to Rome. And as to why you – well, you have three older brothers. Perhaps you may be spared the burden of battle. It would please me very much if you were to become a priest. And so it would be a good thing for you to receive the blessing of the Holy Father, the Pope."

That was a lot to take in. A priest? He wasn't sure about that, not sure at all, so he decided to concentrate on the idea of a journey. It was amazing – he'd never even seen the sea up till now! And as for Rome – he'd heard of it, of course, in tales from long ago, but he'd never thought of it as a real place that you could actually go and see. Where was it – how long would it take to get there? He asked his father.

"It will take many weeks. It will be a long, long journey. But summer is coming, and there will be much to see on the way – much to see and much to learn."

Alfred suddenly thought of something else. He frowned. "But, sir – with you gone, who will look after Wessex?"

"I shall leave it in the care of Aethelbald, of course." He sat down, looking tired. "Fetch me some ale, Alfred, and I'll tell you a little more."

Alfred poured the ale carefully from the jug on the table and carried it to his father where he sat in the carved oak chair by the fire. He didn't much like the idea of Aethelbald being left in charge. Still, he was the oldest, and he was certainly good at fighting people who were smaller than him. Alfred just hoped he'd be as good if he had to fight against the Danes.

The king took the cup from him and drank from it. "I think Wessex is safe for the time being. The pagans need to restore themselves after last year's battle. When they lick their wounds and look about them again – as they will – they'll see that Mercia is weaker than Wessex. Because Mercia has to look both ways – to the Welsh in the west, and the Danes in the east. So they'll go for Mercia and, for a time, Wessex will be safe. And I can look to Rome."

He leaned back in his chair, gazing into the fire and speaking softly. "I'm tired," he said. "I've been fighting for thirty years, and it's long enough. I've wished for some time to go to Rome, to visit the holy places and seek the blessing of the Holy Father. And so we shall go together." He turned towards Alfred again. "You, the youngest of the House of Wessex, and me, the oldest. We shall seek the protection of God against the pagans. For their faces will turn to us one day, Alfred. We shall have to fight them again, and we shall need every bit of help the Church can give us. Might is nothing without right. It's not enough just to sharpen our spears and polish our helmets – we have to know what we are fighting for, we have to be sure that God is with us." He rested his hands on Alfred's shoulders and looked into his eyes seriously. "Do you understand, Alfred?"

"Yes, sir – I – I think so, sir."

But he didn't, not really. If somebody bashed you, you bashed them back. That's what he would do, if he was king. He'd bash the Danes so hard they'd run away and never ever come back.

But he never would be king, would he? Not with three older brothers. No chance.

Rome: 855-6

THE SEA WAS HUGE! Alfred watched in delight as it rippled and churned like a great, gleaming beast with scales of deep blue and emerald green. His ears were filled with the crash of the waves on the shore, and the lapping, licking sound they made against the sides of Cerdic's ship, the *Raven*, and he felt the fine spray on his cheeks and tasted the salt on his lips. It was fantastic!

Cerdic welcomed them proudly onto his ship. He pointed out its lovely curving lines, and Alfred agreed wholeheartedly that it was really more like a swan than a raven.

"Wait till we cast off," Cerdic said seriously. "Then you'll hear her sing. And you'll hear her heart beating!"

It was true. The wind hummed as it filled the sail, and a deeper music came from the *Raven*'s oaken heart, as the timbers shifted beneath their feet. The seabirds swooped and cried as they followed the ship, and behind them the *Raven* left a pathway of foam. Alfred's cheeks flushed, not just with the wind, but with the sheer excitement of it all – and later, when they'd crossed the sea and were sailing up the calmer waters of the River Seine, he sat beside Cerdic and listened with shining eyes to the captain's tales of the places he'd seen. He spoke of frozen lands far to the north, where great white bears prowled among mountains of glittering ice; of desert plains where the people lived in brightly coloured tents and rode on strange animals that carried water in humps on their backs, and of a land where everyone wore silken robes and lived in palaces made of gold.

Alfred listened intently, and wondered if one day he too would see such splendours.

Still, for now, Rome would certainly do.

The River Seine took them to Paris, and then they would have an immensely long journey on horseback, all the way down through Austrasia and Burgundy, till, finally, they would reach Italy. There was so much to see!

There were wide, pale green rivers whose slow waters mirrored the tree-lined banks. Dragonflies flashed among the reeds like darts of emerald and sapphire. In Burgundy there were hills chequered with rows of vines, rolling away to the great plain that the travellers had already crossed. When he got close to the vines, there were bunches of tiny green grapes hanging under the leaves, but they were hard and sour and he spat them out with his eyes smarting. They passed through great forests, much bigger than any they had in Wessex, and Alfred thought he heard the snuffling of boars; he certainly glimpsed deer in the distance, frozen for a moment as they looked and listened and smelt the air, before launching into an exquisitely graceful leap that took them to safety deeper in the forest. Britnoth and others of his father's escort gazed wistfully at the deer, and Alfred hoped they might stop and hunt for their supper, but it was not to be: they mostly slept and ate at monasteries or abbeys, in keeping with the holy purpose of Aethelwulf's journey.

Once or twice, though, they had to camp under the stars when the next abbey was too far away, and those times were the best. Then he could pretend they were on a campaign, and he felt much closer to his father when Aethelwulf and Britnoth and the others sat round the fire and told stories about the campaigns of their youth. He could imagine his father then as a young man, and himself as one of his thegns, or companions.

It was the middle of summer, and weeks had gone by since they'd left Wessex – Alfred had lost track of how many. The further south they went, the hotter it became. Alfred's skin grew as brown as Cerdic's had been, and the sun bleached his brown curls to gold. They weren't used to such heat, and it was a relief to all of them when one day the ground began to rise and the air grew noticeably cooler. Different kinds of trees appeared in the forest: narrow-leaved evergreens tipped with pale green cones.

Then the trees fell away altogether – and they were in a landscape like nothing Alfred had ever seen before. These were mountains, huge and wild and beautiful beyond all imagining: great silver-topped peaks marching one after another far into the distance, till they disappeared into a lilac-coloured haze.

Alfred's eyes widened, and he stopped his pony so he could take it all in. The sun shone brightly but the cool wind ruffled Alfred's hair and stippled icy fingers on his bare arms.

"What are they?" he breathed.

His father studied him, a smile on his face, more interested in looking at his son than at the view. "They're the Alps," he said. "We have to cross them."

Alfred stared. Even though it was summer, he could see that the peaks were tipped with snow. Thin streams tumbled down, exploding into cascades as they glanced off crags and disappeared into dizzying drops.

"But they're so big," he said, bewildered. "How will we ever get to the other side?"

"The road will carry us," said his father. "It will take us over whatever lies in our path – rivers made of ice, ravines so deep you can't even see the bottom – right up to the top of the world. Then it will lead us through a pass and all the way down again into Lombardy. And then before you know it, we'll be in Rome itself!"

Alfred felt doubtful, but his father turned out to be right. He had never seen such a road. There was nothing like it in Wessex, he was quite sure of that. It went exactly where it wanted to go and nothing was able to stop it. Alfred liked its attitude. If there was a river in the way, the road would fling a bridge across it. If there was an inconvenient outcrop of rock, a passage would be cut and the road would blast triumphantly through.

The only thing that puzzled him was that the road didn't go by the shortest way straight up or down, but travelled in a series of loops. When he complained about this, Aethelwulf explained it to him patiently.

"That way, you see, it would be very steep – impossibly so. You might manage it for a bit of the way – say from here to the next loop – but you'd be very tired by the time you got there. And think of the poor horses with all they have to carry – they'd never make it! No, it's much better like this. The ancient Romans built this road, longer ago than anyone can remember, and they knew what they were doing. Sometimes you have to take the longer way to get to where you want to be."

Alfred felt sorry for the packhorses. They were weighed down with all sorts of things – not just the luggage they carried with them for their journey, but the gifts that Aethelwulf had brought for the Pope. Alfred thought it was very kind of his father to be so generous. He wondered if the Pope was very poor, and that was why he needed so much.

When they finally reached Rome, he saw that the Pope wasn't poor at all. How could he be, when he was in charge of such a vast city? He stared at the towering city walls.

"Do you think they'll let us in?" he asked Britnoth, who was riding beside him. He liked Britnoth. Though his dark hair was heavily sprinkled with grey, his eyes twinkled dark, and he was always cheerful and ready with a joke. He smiled now and nodded towards the walls.

"I think you'll find they're not there to keep us out," he said. "With this lot behind us, I imagine we'll be very welcome guests." He pointed with his thumb at the horses behind them with their bulging packs, and Alfred understood. Of course the Romans would be eager for their presents. Who wouldn't be?

They must have been expected, because as they approached, the great gates creaked open, and there to meet them was a party of men on horses: fine, tall horses, with gleaming chestnut coats and silky black manes and tails – very unlike the sturdy, rough-coated little English horses. Alfred leant forward and laid his cheek against his own horse's neck. Its coat felt rough and ticklish, and it had a warm, comfortable smell.

"You're much better than them," he whispered. "You're tough. They're just fancy."

The riders wore elaborate helmets topped with extravagant plumes, and looked disdainfully straight ahead of them, except for the one in front, who spoke in heavily accented English.

"The king of Wessex is welcome in Rome. You will follow me, please."

They wheeled their horses round. They did it beautifully, all together – even the tails all swished at the same time. The men of Wessex followed them through the gates. Lots of people had gathered to watch; some of them seemed to be sniggering as they pointed at the travellers' dusty clothes and unkempt hair. A boy popped his head out of a doorway, and, catching Alfred's eye, stuck out his tongue. When he was sure no one was looking, Alfred pulled his most terrifying face back at him. The boy grinned in appreciation, and Alfred was sorry when they rode on and left him behind. It was a long time since he'd played with anyone his own age.

Aethelwulf suddenly called for a halt and stared around him. He looked awe-struck, and Alfred followed his gaze. The street had widened out into a square, and round it were great buildings supported by massive marble columns, rearing up as if they would touch the sky. Some of the stone might have been crumbling, but Alfred had never seen anything like the huge statues of men and women, with curling hair and powerful muscles and sightless eyes that gazed sadly across the city. They looked as if they too were made of stone, but how could they be? How could anyone have carved stone as if it were softer than wood? Alfred thought there must be magic in it; it was like a city made for and by giants.

Aethelwulf seemed entranced. He dismounted and

sank to his knees, and suddenly he was kissing the earth. Startled and a little embarrassed, Alfred looked round anxiously, hoping the boy hadn't followed them. What was his father thinking of? Thankfully, the king soon stood up again, and his voice rang out clear and strong.

"May we proceed directly to the Basilica? We have travelled long and far, and my heart hungers to gaze on the sacred burial place."

Thoroughly alarmed, Alfred turned to Britnoth and whispered, "Whatever is he talking about? What burial place?"

Britnoth shrugged. "I'm just a simple soldier," he said. "I don't know much. But they do say the grave of Saint Peter himself is in Rome. I suppose he must be buried in this – this basil thing that we're going to."

Alfred was impressed. At home, of course, they had lots of holy relics: bits of material from a saint's cloak, a splinter from St Patrick's staff, sometimes even a whole finger. They were kept safe in precious jewelled reliquaries in monasteries and abbeys, and people would kneel and pray before them, in the hope that the saint would cure their illness, or give them good crops, or protect them on a journey.

But a whole grave – that was unheard of – and St Peter's grave at that! As far as Alfred understood it, Peter was the most important saint of all. He guarded the actual gates of Heaven, and it was his job to decide who was allowed in, and who got thrown to the demons of

Hell, who were said to have a very imaginative range of tortures at their disposal. Alfred swallowed nervously and tried to think holy thoughts in case St Peter was listening.

The Basilica was at the top of a hill – Rome seemed to have lots of hills – and to reach it they had to climb a flight of steps made up of enormous slabs of marble. The steps led to a wide square, which Alfred was by now not surprised to see was also paved with marble. On the far side was a massive brick building topped with a dome. Though Aethelwulf gazed at it with stunned delight, an expression he'd had ever since they entered Rome, Alfred thought it was rather ugly except for the doors, which looked as if they were made of solid silver.

In front of the doors stood a group of men in pure white robes that fell to their ankles in elegant folds. It was obvious that the one in the centre was the most important. The others stood at a respectful distance from him, and he wore a golden cape that glittered in the hot Roman sun. He was a tall man with the powerful build of a fighter, and Alfred squared his shoulders as his father marched him across the square.

"Your Grace," murmured his father, kneeling down to kiss the Pope's ring, "I bring to you my youngest son, Alfred, who may perhaps one day be fortunate enough to join the Church, if God is willing. I hope that you will honour us during our stay by giving him your blessing, and by accepting some small gifts that we have brought with us."

Alfred felt a firm hand on his shoulder and looked up. Pope Leo's expression as he studied Alfred's face was amused and friendly. Alfred began to feel a bit more cheerful at the prospect of joining the Church: it might not be so bad if it had people like this in it.

"So!" smiled the Pope. "The lords of Wessex! You have travelled a great distance, and you are most welcome. Later, you must tell me how things are in your island country – but for now, let us go into the Basilica and give thanks for your safe arrival."

Once inside, Alfred glanced round a little anxiously at the shadowy interior, which soared so high above them he could hardly make out the shape of the dome. He wondered if they would see the saint's grave, or even his actual body, and swallowed nervously.

With considerable relief, he found that they would not. St Peter had been murdered hundreds of years before, when the Romans were still pagans. When they converted to Christianity, they had built the church above his grave. It was still there in a chamber below the altar, but you couldn't see it, though you could peer down a shaft that led directly into the chamber and breathe in the odour of sanctity, as one of the priests reverentially explained to them. Alfred breathed in deeply, and almost choked. It smelled dank and earthy. Was that how holiness smelled?

*　*　*

They were to stay near the Basilica in a house built specially for royal visitors – apparently lots of kings came to Rome to see the Pope. The area was called the Vatican; the Pope lived on the other side, in a palace called the Lateran. As Alfred had noticed, the city was built on hills. They had names that sounded smooth and silky to his ears – the Palatine, the Aventine, the Capitoline, the Janiculum. His own language sounded rough and harsh compared to the tongue of these southerners, and he tried to sound out some of the words he heard them say. Pope Leo heard him and asked if he had been taught any Latin – it would help, he said, because their language was very similar to Latin. Alfred shook his head.

"But I wish I could learn!" he said.

The Pope looked at him thoughtfully. "In times such as these," he said, "there are other skills that are perhaps more important for the sons of kings."

"But I'm not going to be king," explained Alfred, thinking without much enthusiasm about what his father had said about him joining the Church. "I have three older brothers."

"And another who died – Aethelstan, was it not?" The Pope was silent for a moment, and his dark eyes searched Alfred's face. "None of us knows what the future holds, my son. Who can tell what God may ask of you? Perhaps you will be more use to him as a soldier or a lawgiver than a priest." He smiled as Alfred's eyes lit up. "You have an eager mind, Alfred. You must learn to use it, and you can start while you are here."

And he arranged for Alfred to go to the scriptorium and see the work of the scholars. One of them, Brother Anselm, gave Alfred a piece of vellum and showed him how to write his name. Alfred admired the shape of the letters – he thought the "A" with its trail of loops was particularly fine – and set to with a will to copy them. The quill was much harder to control than he'd expected – the ink looked as if a spider had walked through it – but he did it over and over again till at last his "Alfred" was almost as good as Anselm's. Then Anselm took him into the library. He staggered a little as he lifted a huge volume from the shelves and settled it tenderly on a stand. "This is one of our finest books," he said, "and it was written by a scholar from your own island – from Northumbria. Not just copied, mind – he actually wrote it!"

Alfred touched the soft leather cover, and then gasped as Anselm opened it and showed him the first page. It was covered with what seemed at first glance to be the most glorious intricate patterns in jewel-like colours. He stared, entranced.

"Do you see?" smiled Anselm. "These are letters. The title: *Historia Ecclesiastica Gentis Anglorum*. It was written by Bede – the Venerable Bede, we call him, because he lived to a great age and he was full of wisdom."

"What does the title mean, sir? I don't understand it."

Anselm glanced at him. "Oh – no, I suppose you

wouldn't. Perhaps one day you will learn Latin, hmm? You will need it if you want to study..." He suddenly remembered who he was talking to, and became a little flustered. "Ah, no – perhaps – anyway, what it means is, 'The Ecclesiastical History of the English People'. Your people, you see – it's all about your people!"

Alfred wondered if Anselm realized that he was from Wessex, not Northumbria, but thought it might not be polite to point this out. But there was something that puzzled him.

"If it's about the English peoples," he said, "why isn't it in English?"

Anselm looked shocked. "Why, because Latin is the language of learning – of civilization!" Then, perhaps thinking that he might have been tactless, he added kindly, "Though I have heard that the Venerable Bede chose to write some of his books in English, to be sure."

Alfred traced one of the patterns on the page with his finger, his touch gentle and light as a feather.

"I wish I could learn to do this," he said wistfully.

After he'd gone, Brother Anselm carefully put the book away and tidied up his writing tools. An unusual child, he thought to himself: not at all like the usual run of bored and boorish kings and nobles who came to visit the scriptorium because Pope Leo had told them to. He had tried very hard with the quill, and if Anselm was not very much mistaken, he had considerable natural aptitude ... a pity he was who he was, and that he would not be staying in Rome. Anselm would have liked to help him attain his wish.

In the early spring, Aethelwulf decided they must turn towards home. They would make a lengthy stop in Francia, though, he told Alfred, at the court of Charles the Bald, king of the Franks, at Verberie sur Oise, near Paris. Their two families had been allies for several generations, so it would be only courteous, and besides, he said vaguely, he had some business to conclude with Charles.

Judith Martel, Princess of the Franks: 856

ALFRED FELT AWE-STRUCK at being in the presence of Charles the Bald. He was the grandson of the legendary Charlemagne, the Holy Roman Emperor, who had ruled the whole of Europe from the west coast of Francia, east through Carinthia and south through Lombardy – further even than the Wessex party had travelled. Charles cut an impressive figure – with the huge gold helmet-shaped crown on his head, studded with gleaming pearls and rubies the size of pigeons' eggs, how could he not?

Yet there was something Alfred didn't like about the face beneath the crown, and he remembered the stories Britnoth had told him about Charles and his two brothers, Louis and Lothair. Though they were brothers, they hadn't been fond of each other – like him and Baldu, Alfred thought with a twinge of guilt – and when their father died they had squabbled away the Empire, so now Charles only ruled over the western part of it – though that still made him a powerful king.

He liked the look of Charles's daughter, though. She seemed a few years older than Alfred, but still a good deal nearer his age than anyone else he'd spent time with since leaving Wessex. She had dancing dark blue eyes and when she caught his eye her mouth twitched as if she wanted to laugh and she gave him a wink that was so quick he could hardly believe he'd seen it. He watched, fascinated, to see if she'd do it again.

The speeches of welcome seemed to go on so long his legs felt positively itchy with boredom and he had to surreptitiously stand on one leg and try to scratch it with the other one, but at last it was all over and everyone began to move about. He stood on tiptoe, trying to see where Judith had gone, but then suddenly there she was in front of him, grinning.

"I'm Judith," she said, "and you're Alfred, aren't you? The boy who's been to Rome! You are so lucky – I've not been anywhere – well, nowhere half as exciting as that, anyway. Shall we get out of here? It's not much fun, is it… There's lots I can show you, and I want you to tell me all about your travels. Is it true that the Pope's a giant? I've got a hawk called Merlin – we can go and see him if you like … what's the matter? Aren't you coming?"

Alfred felt torn. He was more than happy to go with Judith just about anywhere she wanted to go, but he didn't know if he ought to stay with his father. They had been almost everywhere together in the months away from Wessex, and... Judith listened to him as he explained, her dark gold head slightly to one side, her darkly lashed eyes quizzical.

"I'm sure it's all right," she said. "But just to make sure, I'll ask your father myself."

She flitted over to Aethelwulf, who bent his silvery head to listen to her. He glanced across at Alfred and nodded. And then Aethelwulf watched her with a smile on his face as she threaded her way back through the crowd to tell Alfred triumphantly that all was well – his father said he was free to go and enjoy himself.

That was the thing about Judith. She made people happy. She made people smile.

Judith wanted to show Alfred everything. The grounds of Charles's palace were full of flower gardens, apple orchards and a large fish pond, but Alfred's favourite place was a walled garden where vegetables and herbs grew. Peach, cherry, mulberry and plum blossoms were scattered like pink and white stars on trees whose branches were trained to lie flat against the stone walls and soak up the warmth of the sun. Usually they had the garden to themselves, and they would spend hours talking. Judith was as curious about the world as Alfred was, and she wanted to hear all about Wessex. She asked about his brothers, and her face softened when he told her that he could hardly remember his mother. Her own mother, Ermentrude, was a forceful woman who was far more interested in her sons and her husband than her daughter, but Judith didn't seem to mind.

"She doesn't care what I do," said Judith cheerfully, "so mostly I just do as I please."

She was keen to hear about Rome. "Is it very beautiful?" she asked eagerly.

Alfred thought about this. "Some bits are," he said finally. "Some of it's really old. There's one great big round building, several storeys high. They say it's where the Roman emperors used to make the Christians fight lions, and all the people were allowed to watch. And there's a huge archway, with carvings on it. And there are statues lying about all over the place."

"Statues of what?" she asked.

Alfred frowned, trying to remember. "Mostly they're just of men and women – great big ones – but some of them are of monsters. There was one of a woman's head, only with snakes instead of hair. And a woman with a helmet. She looked very fierce. Oh, and the one I liked best, of a wolf and two boys. The wolf was like their mother. They were called Romulus and Remus, and they were the founders of Rome. I did ask Brother Anselm about them, but he wouldn't tell me much – he said they were mostly to do with pagan gods and goddesses, and really there was no place for them in today's Rome. A lot of them were broken – sometimes you'd see just an arm or a leg lying at the edge of the road. But some of them were beautiful, especially the horses. They looked so real

41

you'd think they could move."

"Who was Brother Anselm?"

Alfred told her about Anselm and the library, and his one writing lesson. Judith looked at him, surprised.

"Do you mean you don't know how to write?"

Alfred shook his head. "And I can't read either," he admitted. Her astonishment made it obvious that she could, and he felt embarrassed.

"But that's terrible! There are so many books here, beautiful books, full of stories." Her face lit up. "If you stay long enough, I can teach you to read them ... or perhaps you should go to the palace school."

Alfred was puzzled. At his father's court, of course, there were poets and storytellers, and monks who read to his father from books, but the only people who actually learned to read and write lived in monasteries.

"What do you mean?" he asked. "What's the palace school?"

"My great-grandfather, Charlemagne, set it up," she explained. "He said there should be schools for everyone. He invited people from all over Europe to come here, to advise him and pass on their skills, and they did, and not just to him but to others as well. There were scholars, artists, musicians, poets ... it must have been marvellous then," she said wistfully.

Alfred looked round. "Isn't it marvellous now?" he asked.

"Yes, but – well, Father's always falling out with people.

And there are the Vikings."

Always, everywhere, people talked of the Vikings, with a catch in the voice, and a hint of fear in the eyes.

"They attacked Paris ten years ago. It's not far from here, you know. They could get here quite easily if they decided to, up the Seine and along the Oise. My father paid them to go away, and they did. But I sometimes wonder if they'll come back," said Judith, pulling the petals off a sprig of cherry blossom.

"Don't worry – I'll fight them for you!" declared Alfred, jumping up and thrashing the air with a pretend sword.

And she laughed, and said that made her feel ever so much better.

Alfred told Judith about the woods of Wessex, particularly the ones in the summer country, where the hunting was good, and she decided she must show him the great Forest of Compiegne, which lay just to the north of Verberie. Much to Judith's disgust, her father said they could not go unaccompanied, and he sent a young man to ride with them. Baldwin was seventeen, tall and broad shouldered, with cropped dark hair and serious grey eyes.

"I don't think he likes being a nursemaid to us!" whispered Judith to Alfred, her eyes sparkling with laughter. Alfred didn't need a nursemaid, and he looked resentfully at the newcomer.

Baldwin had come to court to go the palace school.

But as well as learning about philosophy and poetry and music, he was learning to be a soldier. Alfred had missed his sessions with his brother, Aethelred, and with his father's old armourer, who had stayed at home in Wessex, and was delighted when he found that Baldwin could be persuaded to spar with him.

Baldwin was determined to instill in him the importance of balance. He made him walk along a branch bridging a stream in the woods, balancing a long pole in his hands. Judith thought it was all very amusing, and threw stones into the water to startle him and make him fall in. Baldwin smiled, but spoke gravely to Alfred.

"In battle, balance is crucial. Think. You're on a horse, and you have a lance in your hand, and you bury it in your enemy. Then what do you do?"

"I pull it out!"

"Do you? We'll try it. Tomorrow."

The next day, Baldwin brought a small lance and a sack of hay. He gave the lance to Alfred, and positioned the sack on the other side of the clearing. Then he stood back.

"Now. As fast as you can. That sack's your enemy – it's a Viking, and he's going to kill you unless you can kill him first."

Alfred settled himself firmly in the saddle and glared fiercely at the sack.

"When my arm goes down! NOW!"

Alfred charged. But it was difficult to control his horse

44

and keep the lance steady. He missed the sack. The lance flopped harmlessly onto the ground and he veered off to the left. If it hadn't been for the stirrups, he would have fallen off.

"Do it again," said Baldwin. "You're not holding it properly. Try it like this. And remember – if you don't kill him, he'll kill the princess, too." There was a little intake of breath from Judith.

Alfred clenched his teeth, his fingers, his whole body, and charged again. This time he did better – he thrust the lance into the sack. But he did it so hard that when the lance stopped, so did he. The horse carried on. Alfred whirled through the air in what felt like a perfect arc – and found himself flat on his back.

"Ouch!" he groaned. With a rare grin, Baldwin was standing above him, pointing his sword at Alfred's chest.

"Trouble is," he said, "there's always another Viking. Balance," he continued. "Without it, you won't stay on your horse and you won't be able to control your weapon, whatever it is."

"I want to try!" said Judith. She ran over to the branch, still in place above the stream. Then she held her skirts up a little, and with her back straight and her chin high, she walked delicately across. Then, laughing triumphantly, she turned to come back.

"Be careful!" called Baldwin anxiously. "The branch is slippery!" She grinned, and put one foot carefully in front of the other. Alfred, who was sore and bruised, felt a

45

little annoyed. It hadn't bothered Baldwin when he'd fallen in!

She had almost reached their side of the stream when a bird flew up, rattling the leaves and starting her. She wobbled, and Baldwin rushed closer to the edge and held out his hands to grasp hers and steady her. He held her eyes, too, with his own. And Alfred was puzzled to see that they didn't let go of each other's hands, even when Judith was safely on firm ground again.

One day, when they had been at the Frankish court for several months, Alfred was waiting at the gate that led to the falconry. He and Judith were going to take her favourite hawk out hunting.

He'd already been waiting for some time, and he was beginning to wonder if she had forgotten. He hopped from one foot to the other, feeling a bit silly. He decided to count to ten three times, and if she hadn't come by then he would go and look for her.

He counted three times, and then two more times for luck, but still she wasn't there, so he set off back to the castle. No one seemed to know where she was. Puzzled, he thought for a moment. Perhaps she was in the walled garden?

In the centre of the garden was a small fountain surrounded by a pool. It was edged with a low wall. Alfred thought the fountain was wonderful: he was fascinated by the way the water had somehow been persuaded to

46

run uphill, just so that it could then come splashing down again. He'd asked Judith how it worked, but she'd laughed at him and said she had no idea, it wasn't something she'd ever thought to ask anyone.

And there she was, sitting on the wall, gazing into the water with her back to him. She was very still. Her head was drooping, as if she couldn't be bothered to hold it up, and her shoulders were oddly hunched.

Alfred hesitated. He felt worried and he didn't know quite what to do. Something was wrong, he could tell without even seeing her face. What could it be? He'd never seen her sad. Cross, sometimes, like when her mother had told her she must stay indoors and do some sewing instead of running wild in the woods and grounds – but never sad.

He went closer, and sat down beside her.

"Judith?" he said timidly.

She stiffened slightly, but didn't look at him. She said something, but her voice was muffled. He leant closer.

"Judith? I didn't hear."

Then she turned to face him, and he flinched. Her face was shiny, her mouth trembling, her eyes puffy and red.

"Did you know?" she demanded angrily.

"Know what?"

"That I'm to marry your father!"

He stared at her. What was she saying? How could that be true? She must have made a mistake.

"What do you mean?" he said stupidly.

"My father told me this morning. It's to – to seal the alliance between Wessex and Francia. We are to be married in three weeks' time, and then I'm to go back to Wessex with you. Away from here and – and everything."

"But – but – " Alfred groped helplessly for words. Judith was his friend, not much older than he was. Aethelwulf was his father, dearly loved, but his beard was white and he was old. How could this be? An impossible thought occurred to him. If Judith married his father, did that mean she would become his mother?

He heard the sound of the gate opening – someone was coming into the garden. Judith looked up.

It was Baldwin, and he looked stricken. For a moment, Alfred stood there awkwardly, waiting. But no one seemed to notice or care that he was there, and so he turned and trailed out of the garden.

The marriage took place in October, and at the same time, Judith was crowned Queen of Wessex. Alfred watched as the archbishop of Reims carefully lowered the gold crown onto her head. Immediately afterwards, Aethelwulf took his new bride by the hand and showed her to the congregation. Her face was pale, but she was smiling, and she searched out Alfred and gave him a special look which said not to worry, it was going to be all right.

And it would be, just about. After that morning in the garden, he had thought for a long time and then gone to find his father in the palace. Aethelwulf knew why he had come.

"It is a matter of state, Alfred," he said quietly. "It is to seal the alliance between Francia and Wessex. Judith can be your mother or she can be your friend, as you and she wish. She will be the queen, and she will be an honoured member of our household. But ... I have enough sons already. More than enough, perhaps," he sighed.

Alfred was puzzled. What did having enough sons have to do with it? And what did he mean by "more than enough"?

The last part became clearer over the weeks that followed. Baldu was stirring up unrest in Wessex. There were disturbing rumours that he was trying to take his father's place on the throne. As soon as the wedding was over, they would return. They had been away for too long.

It was raining when they set off on their way back to Wessex, and a light grey drizzle blotted out the coast of Francia almost as soon as they had left it. Judith sat with Alfred in the stern of the boat. She didn't turn to look at what she was leaving, but she held Alfred's hand so tightly it almost hurt. He looked at her anxiously. She was staring straight ahead, towards her new country.

"I will go back," she said, so quietly he could hardly

hear her above the noise of the sea and the ship and the wind. "This isn't for ever."

Alfred was sorry for her sadness. But some hours later, when the clouds parted to let a few rays of sunshine light up the distant coastline of Wessex, his heart lifted and his face broke into a smile. To Judith, it might seem like exile, but to him, it was home. Soon he'd see Redi again.

And Baldu. His father was very angry with Baldu. Still, the king would sort things out, just as he always did. His mind switched back to Judith. He did so hope she would be happy.

Partings: 860

WAS IT REALLY only five years since they'd come back from Rome and Francia? It seemed impossible: so much had happened. Alfred thought back to how he had felt that day. He'd been excited to be home, but Judith had been sad. He shivered.

He crouched down on the beach now, plunging his hands into the pebbles and letting them trickle through his fingers. Judith was going home. He was glad for her, especially after all that had happened, but he would miss her greatly. He glanced back along the road: no sign of her yet. Her train, laden down with baggage, had travelled more slowly from Winchester than he and Redi on their swift horses. It would be a while yet before she arrived. Redi was down at the water's edge, talking to the ship's captain.

The pebbles were smooth and cool between his fingers, glistening with seawater. No matter how many he scooped up, there were always more, and always would be.

They didn't change, but other things did. People did. They came, and they went. They lived, and then they died.

When the king had found out five years ago that the rumours were true, and that Baldu had been plotting against him, his shoulders had sagged and his eyes had turned bleak, like the sea on a cold winter's day. Baldu tried to make excuses: he said he had thought his father was tired, and wanted to lay down the burden of government. He only wanted to help, he said, his voice a resentful whine, as it so often was. But nobody believed him. The truth was that Baldu wanted power, and he wasn't prepared to wait for it.

There was more. People said that when Baldu was told about his father's impending marriage to Judith, his eyes had shot flames and he'd foamed at the mouth. Alfred wasn't sure he quite believed that, but it was certainly true that Baldu didn't like Judith. He was always staring at her, in a nasty way that made Alfred feel like standing between them to protect her, preferably with a big sword in his hand. He'd talked to Redi about it, and Redi had sighed.

"He's jealous, Alfred," Redi had said. "He's eaten up by jealousy. First he was jealous of you, because he thought you were Father's favourite, and now he's afraid Judith will have children, and Father will love them better too."

Alfred was astonished. He didn't know whether he

was more surprised that anyone thought he was Aethelwulf's favourite, or that Baldu could think that Judith and his father would have children. And anyway, hadn't his father said when they were in Francia that he already had enough sons?

The king hadn't banished Baldu, as many people thought he should have done. He'd tried to make peace with him by sending him to the far west of Wessex, to rule it as his own. Baldu was out of sight, and mostly out of mind.

Once he was gone, everything was much better. Judith was much quieter than before, but she seemed reasonably content: anyone could see she was fond of Aethelwulf.

Aethelwulf treated her like a much loved daughter, and to Alfred, she was an older sister and a best friend all rolled into one. He had the people he loved around him, and he was happy.

But then, two years after their marriage, Alfred's father was thrown from his horse. At first, it seemed as though he would recover. He couldn't put his weight on his foot but, with rest, he was expected to get better.

Instead, he developed a fever. His eyes grew frighteningly bright, and darted restlessly about, and his fingers plucked at things in the air that no one else could see. He didn't realize that Alfred was there, and he spoke to people who had died long ago. Pain sat like a stone in Alfred's chest, as his father drifted further and further away from them.

Messages were sent to Baldu and Aethelbert. Alfred hardly knew Aethelbert, because he had been in the east for many years, acting as his father's regent in Kent, Surrey and Sussex.

Baldu arrived first. He came with a large body of horsemen, looking tense and excited. He swept into the king's bedchamber, but he scarcely even looked at his father. Instead, his eyes travelled up and down Judith's body in an insolent, sneering way that made Alfred want to hit him. But Alfred was only a boy, and it was Redi who stood in front of Judith and told Baldu to get out if he did not know how to treat the king and queen with proper respect.

Baldu laughed, a cruel, mocking laugh, and said that was fine, he could wait. It wouldn't be long, he said, casting a contemptuous glance towards his father, lying unconscious on his bed.

And it wasn't. Aethelwulf grew weaker and weaker, and then faintly, almost imperceptibly, his breathing slowed and then finally stopped. Alfred felt numb with grief, but there was no time to mourn because Baldu immediately took control of the palace – and it was his right to do so, because Aethelwulf's will stated that Aethelbert was to rule the eastern shires, but Baldu was to rule the rest of Wessex. They were all his subjects now.

They had to accept that. But his next move was one

that stunned and horrified everyone. He put Redi and Alfred under guard, then seized Judith. For days nobody saw her, and Alfred was frantic with worry. Then Baldu announced that he and Judith had been secretly married. Alfred stared in horror and disbelief. Judith's face was strained and white, with a huge purple bruise on one cheek. But the worst thing was her eyes – like the eyes of a dead thing.

Alfred clenched his fists and started forward, but Redi held him by the arm.

"Don't!" he said. "He's the king. He can do what he wants. There's nothing we can do. Not now." His voice was bleak and his face was hard.

How could this be right? How could it?

It was the beginning of a terrible time for Wessex. But within three years, Baldu too was dead, apparently ambushed by a Danish raiding party. That was what was said, though no one seemed to have heard of these particular raiders either before or after. The only evidence was Baldu's body, and his wounds didn't speak. He'd made many enemies, and now he was gone. Aethelbert returned from Kent to rule the whole of Wessex, and the people breathed a collective sigh of relief.

Alfred heard the sound of horses. He walked back up the shore, his feet crunching in the pebbles, and helped Judith from her horse. The wind tugged at her dark gold hair. There were hollows in her cheeks and shadows behind her dark blue eyes, but her smile was bright enough to light up the whole day.

"Don't be sad," she said gently. "Look, I have a present for you."

Surprised, he took the package from her. It was rectangular, quite heavy, and wrapped in linen. He gasped when he opened it. Inside was a book; the cover was decorated with gold leaf, and the clasp was studded with garnets and inlaid with enamel. He opened it, and his eyes widened. It was so beautiful! Dragons' heads writhed, their breath spiralling out in curls of flame, and as he looked, he began to see other creatures where at first he had seen only intricately interlaced patterns. Words looped across the fine vellum pages – if only he knew what they meant!

"I'm going to learn to read it," he said with determination.

"Yes," she grinned. "You must! It's in your language. I thought that would be easier than Latin. You *should* know how to read," she added more seriously. "How I wish I had the time to teach you! Books are so important, Alfred. They have ideas in them, knowledge, wisdom, stories about people who've gone before. Learn to read this, and I'll send you others, I promise!"

Then she leant forward and her lips brushed his cheek.

Unable to speak, he hugged her. But the ship was waiting and she had to go. He stood and watched until it became a tiny smudge in the distance, and finally faded into the blue horizon, and he hardly knew whether the wetness on his cheeks was tears, or just the spray from the waves crashing relentlessly onto the shingle. She had gone.

Then Redi touched him on the shoulder, and together they trudged back up the beach.

Strange Meeting: 863

A LFRED WAS LOST. He really didn't see how he could be, because he'd only left the lodge at Athelney twenty minutes ago, but he had no idea which way back. He took a deep breath. This is ridiculous, he told himself firmly. All I have to do is go back the way I came, and I'll be on the path again.

Alfred turned round, and was immediately confronted by a thick belt of thorn and alder. Impossible. He turned back, and began to push his way through the under-growth where it seemed thinnest. He had to hold the pliant, springy stems out of the way, and when he let them go to move forward, one of them whipped him sharply across the face. He let out an involuntary cry, and felt a warm trickle of blood on his cheek.

He was cross with himself. Was this how he was going to show his brothers that he was ready for his first com-mand, by whimpering at a scratch? Then he felt angry with them all over again, remembering what had happened.

He'd stormed out of the lodge, needing to be outside and away from them with their caution and their carefulness. He would go hunting. He'd bring back a deer which he would sling contemptuously at their feet, to prove he was a man of action, and they were just ditherers.

It was, by all accounts, only a small band of raiders. With just a few men Alfred could have been halfway there by now, and in no time at all, there would have been one bunch of Vikings who'd never see their ship again. But no. "We don't know for sure how many there are," Aethelbert had said. "Best to send someone experienced." Someone old, that was what he meant. He was so sensible, so dull! But it wasn't just him – even Redi, who knew how much Alfred wanted to prove himself, had just grinned and ruffled his hair, and said, "Patience, little brother, patience. Your time will come."

Forgetting the pain, he looked round impatiently. It looked lighter in one direction, and there seemed to be a patch of green through the network of branches and twigs, though it was difficult to see clearly because everything was smudged and softened by fine grey drizzle. More carefully this time, he used his knife to cut a way through the bushes, and emerged with relief back onto the path.

Just as he was deciding which way to go, he heard something rustling in the undergrowth. He swung round, instantly alert, reaching for his bow and pulling an arrow from his belt. By the time he'd completed the turn and caught a glimpse of a pale brown flank, the arrow was ready to go, and he loosed it, feeling that familiar sense of triumph and release as it streaked through the air to plunge into its victim.

There was a little sound, a cry of bewilderment and pain, and then the deer was gone, plunging through the undergrowth with Alfred crashing eagerly after it.

Eventually the trees became more widely spaced and he found himself in a clearing. The rain had stopped, and a few rays of sunshine found their way between the leaves, forming a pool of pale gold dappled light which shifted and swayed with the movement of the branches. He blinked and rubbed his eyes. Sweat had run into them, and he was at first unsure of what he was seeing.

There was a girl, sitting on the ground in the pool of light. A deer lay beside her – his deer, the one he'd shot. Its head was in her lap, and she was stroking it gently, tenderly.

"That's mine," said Alfred sharply.

She looked at him. She had dark hair, shiny like a bird's wing, and her eyes were strange, he noticed, very pale, almost silvery. She moved a little and Alfred saw with a sharp twinge of shame that the deer was in fawn. He'd been careless. It was one of the first rules you learned; you never, ever shot a breeding mother.

The girl said nothing, but there was something about her level gaze that made him feel angry and defiant.

60

Who did she think she was? What was it to do with her?

"I said it's mine," he said again. "And this is my family's land. I can do what I want here. Do you *know* who I am?"

She ignored him, until he asked her name.

Then she looked at him, a long cool look that seemed to flow into his soul, and said, "My name is Cerys. And you are Prince Alfred."

Then she bent her head, her hair falling over her face so he could no longer see those disturbing eyes, and she began to speak. Her words were in a different language, lilting, more like music than speech. As he listened, something was happening to the air. It began to weave itself into veils of white mist, which wrapped themselves round him, touching his face like cool damp fingers. It grew thicker, and thicker again, and he thought he cried out as the world disappeared leaving nothing, nothing but blankness…

He didn't know how long it was before he came to. When he did, both girl and doe were gone. He picked up his bow, and found his way without any difficulty back to the lodge. He felt clumsy and careless and somehow deeply ashamed, and it was a very long time before he told anyone what had happened that day.

Next in Line: 868

A GREAT FEAST was being prepared to celebrate the visit of Alfred's sister, Aethelswith, and her husband Burgred, the king of Mercia. Alfred hardly knew Aethelswith: she'd gone away to be married when he was very small, and they had only seen each other occasionally since then. This visit wasn't a social one: Burgred was coming to finalize a treaty with Redi, who had been king for three years now since Aethelbert had died while fighting against the Danes in Kent.

It had been the usual story: the Northmen had made a treaty with the men of Kent, and promised to leave them in peace. Aethelbert had sweetened the treaty with an offer of money, but the Danes had evidently concluded that they'd get richer by attacking Kent, so they had broken camp in the night, taking Aethelbert by surprise. He died later of his wounds, and Redi became king, with Alfred his second in command. Alfred hadn't been close to Aethelbert, though he had grown fond of him;

Aethelbert could sometimes be pompous, but he was kind. There was no time to grieve: they must always keep their minds on the Northmen – what they were doing and where they would strike next.

Meat was roasting, venison and beef and pork, and Alfred's mouth watered at the rich and succulent smell. They would eat well tonight, but he decided he couldn't wait, and set off in search of a hunk of bread and cheese. Hylda was carrying a basket full of bread ready to be served to the guests when they arrived, as was the custom, and she smacked his hand as he helped himself. He might be the king's brother, a grown man of nineteen and a battle-hardened fighter, but to her he was still the little boy she'd looked after all those years ago.

He dodged her, laughing, and bit appreciatively into the warm bread. The hall was full of servants, laying sweet smelling rushes on the floor, getting the tables ready and making sure that the candles were fresh.

As he stood watching, something caught his eye. It was a girl. Or at least, it wasn't the girl herself that he noticed; it was her hair, which fell loosely down her back. It was so dark it was almost black. It reminded him of something, and he felt instantly on edge. He frowned, trying to capture the memory, and without thinking about what he was doing, went across to her and touched her on the shoulder.

She turned, and he thought, *Why, she doesn't have silver eyes!* And then he remembered a girl in a wood. She had puzzled him, and she'd made him feel ashamed. But this wasn't her. This was just a servant girl. Mumbling something, he backed away, and the girl put her hand to her mouth and giggled. He stumbled into a bench, so that people turned to see what was happening. It was all getting very embarrassing, when fortunately there was a commotion outside and he realized the Mercian party must have arrived. He stood up with as much dignity as he could muster, tugged his tunic straight and strode out of the hall, ignoring the laughter that travelled after him.

And then he saw her. She wasn't the silver-eyed girl – of course she wasn't. That girl was far away to the west, in the woods and marshes of the summer country. This girl had dark eyes, calm and tranquil. She sat still on her horse, waiting for someone to help her down. Her ash brown hair nestled in glossy curls round her neck. Her skin had a glow about it, with cheeks flushed rose by the spring sun and lips that looked as if they would feel like petals if you could only touch them. Her dress was blue, *like the sky*, he thought. Something tugged faintly at his memory.

Her mouth curved into an uncertain smile, and he realized he was staring. He walked across to her, and held up his arms, placing his hands on either side of her waist and lifting her down. He didn't notice the satisfied look that passed between his sister and his brother. He didn't notice anything, except Ealswith.

Her mother was related to Burgred, and her father was an ealdorman in Mercia. Her marriage to Alfred would strengthen the alliance between Mercia and Wessex. But to Alfred, none of that mattered. All that mattered was that when he looked at her, he felt as if he was coming home.

A year had passed, and Alfred was gazing fondly at his daughter. They'd named her Aethelfled, but that seemed much too long a name for so small a child, so they called her Fleda. He and Ealswith had brought her outside, so that she could lie in the summer sunshine, kicking her feet and blinking at the leaves of the old oak tree that rustled above her.

"Look at her hands," he said to Ealswith, marvelling. "Her fingers are so tiny, but everything's perfect – just look at her nails!"

"Of course she's perfect," said Ealswith with some satisfaction. "She's our daughter."

He laughed, and then looked up as a shadow fell across them. It was Oswald, one of his thegns. He looked apologetic and a little embarrassed.

"I'm sorry to – to interrupt, my lord," he said, "but the king asks if you could come to the council chamber. There is a deputation of farmers here, and the king would like your advice."

"Farmers?" said Alfred, jumping up lightly. "I don't know much about planting and suchlike. I shouldn't think I'll be much use. But I'll come, all the same." He kissed the top of Ealswith's head, and waved to Fleda, who quite clearly, he thought, waved back at him. Oswald waited patiently, and Alfred grinned.

"What's up, Oswald? Wait till you're a father yourself – then you'll understand!"

"Yes, my lord – no doubt," muttered Oswald.

"Why are these farmers here?"

"It's the levy, my lord. They say that too many men are being called up to fight, and they won't be able to get the harvest in. Last year was bad, and they say this one will be worse, because the weather hasn't been right and because some of them had to use the seed they'd saved for sowing to feed their families."

"Oh, farmers!" said Alfred impatiently. "They always find something to complain about. It rains too much, it doesn't rain enough... If we don't have enough men to defend the kingdom, they won't get any crops at all because the Danes will take everything – have they thought of that?"

Fired up with indignation, he strode into the palace and through the great hall, with Oswald following. By the time they reached the council chamber, the tender father had disappeared, and the face the farmers saw was that of a soldier, grim and determined.

Aethelred briefly explained the farmers' request, and Alfred listened, watching his brother's face. He could see that Aethelred had sympathy with the farmers' case. Redi could always see both sides to a question: it wasn't necessarily a useful quality in a king, though it was a lovable one in a brother. Alfred saw things more clearly, and was decisive about what was most important. Their differences made them a good team: they worked well together.

He turned to look at the farmers. There were four of them. They looked on edge and nervous, fidgeting with the hats they held in their hands, and glancing uneasily at the circular room, hung with tapestries and dominated by the round table. Only their spokesman seemed comfortable: he was tall and lean, with silver hair and pale grey eyes. He ignored his surroundings but watched the king and his brother closely.

"May I suggest something?" said Alfred abruptly. He stared at the tall man, feeling slightly irritated by the other's level gaze. "We must have the men. It is your duty to fight for your lord – of that there is no question. Nor is there any question of the need. The Danish army is bigger than anything you've ever seen – they have thousands of men. They've overrun the north and they're about to do the same to Mercia. They've not turned to us yet because they know we're strong, but it's only a matter of time. Do you know what they did to the king of Northumbria? They call it the blood eagle. They cut open his back – while he lived – cut out his ribs and spread out his lungs like wings. They do it as a tribute to their gods. Nasty, isn't it?"

The men were transfixed, staring at him in horror, all except one who had turned very white and looked as if he was going to be sick, and the leader, whose gaze was still cool and considering. Alfred could hear Aethelred shifting in his seat behind him, and knew his brother thought he'd gone too far. But he had a point to make.

"Nothing is more important than stopping the Danes – *nothing*! But the king is not deaf to what you say. We can release seed from the royal granaries, to make sure there's enough to plant for next year."

He turned, and took the seat beside the king.

"So be it," said Aethelred.

But unbelievably, the farmers' leader was speaking again.

"There may not be enough people left to sow seed for next year," he said, barely courteous. "The children and the old people are already weak. Spring came late and there has not been enough rain. The yield will be poor, and every hand will be needed to bring it in. The men are needed on the land!"

Alfred sprang up angrily, but Aethelred put a restraining hand on his arm.

"The times are hard," said the king evenly. "When we put the Danes to flight, it will be time enough to live more gently. For now, we need fighters. However, I will give orders to release all the grain we can to help you, and we will ease the restrictions on hunting in the royal forests for the next few months. Now you may go."

Before he turned to go, the grey-eyed man gave Alfred one last long glance. A memory stirred in Alfred of a more silvery gaze, but he shrugged it off. He was a grown man now, and there was no space in his life for mysterious mists and silver-eyed girls. He had all the enchantment he needed from Ealswith and their daughter.

Aethelred raised an eyebrow at him.

"What?" said Alfred.

"The blood eagle? Do we *know* that happened?"

Alfred shrugged again. "It might have. People say it did. If the Northmen haven't done it yet, they probably will when they hear the stories."

"Are we better than them, Alfred?" said Aethelred quietly.

"Of course we are! You know that!"

"Then we should behave as if we are. The truth matters. Don't start to forget that."

Alfred's face softened. "You should have been a priest, Redi. You are too good for this life."

The king, his brother, smiled. "But we couldn't choose, could we? We do what we are given to do, as well as we can. Just as those farmers do."

"Yes. We do what we have to do. We rule, and they do as we tell them."

"And?"

"And we try to do God's will."

"Yes. And now I am going to pray, so that I'll be as sure

as I can be that what we do is indeed God's will."

Alfred watched him go, bewildered. How could it not be God's will to put everything they had into protecting Wessex from the Danes? Surely it was obvious? Only last year, they'd been called north to Nottingham to stand with Burgred against the Northmen. The call could come again at any time and, when it did, they had to be ready.

He shrugged, and went to find Ealswith and Fleda. He would spend time with them while he could, and then he'd fight when it was necessary. He felt sorry for Redi. Life seemed so much more complicated to him. Perhaps it was just something that happened as you got older.

The Year of Battles: 871

ALFRED WIPED THE SWEAT from his head with the back of his hand and felt the texture of something gritty pressing into his skin. He caught a powerful whiff of his body, unwashed in weeks. Stale blood, his and that of others, had soaked into his mail shirt. There had been so many battles, so much fighting. He saw a clump of pale yellow primroses near his foot, and stared at them in astonishment. Was it really still spring?

He was leaning against a tall beech tree, away from the field of battle. Its trunk was smoothly fluted like one of the marble columns he'd seen a lifetime ago in Rome, and its fresh young leaves rustled, sifting the April sunlight. He closed his eyes, feeling the blessed warmth on his eyelids, and allowed himself to sink down until he was sitting on the ground.

It was over. It must be over. He opened his eyes again and let his gaze drift wearily over the battlefield. So many more men dead. How long could they go on? Was

God angry with them? He remembered Ashdown. As the day began, Redi had been hearing Mass in his tent. Alfred had sent messengers to press his brother to make haste, but the reply had come back that the king's duty was to God first and, finally losing patience, Alfred had given the impetuous order to advance. And that day, the battle had been theirs. He smiled, remembering. He'd felt joyous and triumphant, and convinced that this was the beginning of the end for the Danes. Redi had smiled, that sweet sardonic smile, and said that it was all thanks to God, who must have listened to his prayers.

But this didn't feel like victory. He could hear the groans of the wounded, see the blood mingled with mud and smeared on the flesh of the broken bodies, smell the awful charnel house smell.

Then he heard something else. A hum that became a rumble and developed into a roar. He sprang to his feet and shaded his eyes to look towards the origin of the sound, on the ridge to the south. Oswald was there beside him.

"It's another army!" said Oswald in disbelief.

They could see the outline of many men – hundreds, thousands of men – and the telltale glint of weapons and shields.

"The king is over there," whispered Alfred. "Right in their path!"

Galvanized, he roared to everyone who could stand to grab their shields and make for the king. He forgot his weariness and ran, careless of where he trod, till the breath felt as if it was being torn from his chest.

The fighting had already begun by the time they reached the foot of the ridge. Alfred swung his sword like a madman, cutting through everything in his way until he caught sight of his brother, recognizable by the cynehelm, the royal helmet gleaming with gold. Aethelred was fighting a huge Danish warrior with flying blond hair, who seemed to be laughing as he wielded the biggest sword Alfred had ever seen. Oswald, beside him, gasped, and muttered, "Who on God's sweet earth is *that?*"

And at that moment, Aethelred let out a groan, and sank to his knees. The tall Dane withdrew his sword from the upper part of the king's chest, and raised it ready for the final blow. Summoning every last vestige of energy he possessed, Alfred hurtled towards him and put up his own sword to parry the blow. Taken by surprise, the Dane stumbled, but was soon ready again, balanced lightly for such a big man. For a moment, they stood facing each other. The Dane's gaze flickered to Aethelred, lying groaning on the ground, and he spoke, his accent sounding strange and guttural to the men of Wessex.

"You're only a boy, but you're brave. Take your king. He's going to die. Take him, and then run somewhere and hide. Because I am Guthrum!" He looked round him as if waiting for something, and his men roared a cheer of assent. He smiled cheerily at Alfred. "I'll be in touch. I *might* go away. But you'll have to pay me. Go and tell your king's council that – tell them they'll have to dig deep into their pockets!" He turned and began to move off, giving orders to his men, who fanned out and began to move through the bodies, casually despatching the wounded from both sides.

But Alfred wasn't watching. He was on his knees beside Redi.

"You're not going to die!" he muttered furiously. "I won't let you!"

They carried the king to where the horses were tethered, and laid him carefully in a cart to carry him back to the palace at Chippenham.

The tall Dane had been right. Aethelred had lost too much blood. He grew weaker and weaker, then became feverish. Soon after Easter he died.

Alfred, the last of all his brothers, was now the king of Wessex.

He knew that, for the moment, he would have to pay the danegeld – the tribute that so many kings all over Europe had to pay to make the Danes leave them in peace. After nine exhausting battles in one year, he didn't have the manpower left to do anything else. He hated it, but for the present he had no choice.

After the Danes had left Wessex and gone north, Alfred

went into the chamber where his daughter lay sleeping. He knelt beside her bed. He was struck by how peaceful she was, and how beautiful. He listened to the sound of her breathing, soft and steady, one small intake of air after another. She didn't know it, but she depended on him to keep her safe – they all did.

It seemed to him that he had never seen anything as lovely as the curve of her dark eyelashes resting on the softness of her cheek, and he touched her hair very gently, letting one golden curl wind itself round his finger.

"Up till now," he said very quietly, "everyone I've ever loved has either died or gone away. Now my last brother's gone, the best of all of us. And so I'm king. And from this day on, so help me, God, I'm going to keep the people safe, and I'm going to keep you safe. I will find a way. No matter what it takes."

Ealswith stood unseen, leaning against the doorway, her hand resting lightly on the great curve of her stomach. And her heart wept for the loneliness in his voice.

FLEDA'S STORY

Seven years have passed. After a few years' respite, the Danes have returned to Wessex, as both Guthrum and Alfred knew they would. First, the Northmen go to Wareham, on the south coast. Alfred manages to contain them, but is unable to do more than that. Each side takes hostages, and a truce is sworn.

But Guthrum slaughters his hostages, breaks out and goes further along the coast to Exeter. Again, they make terms. This time, Guthrum swears on holy relics that he will abide by the truce. Despite this, he breaks it as he breaks every promise. Alfred shadows him as he rides north: eventually Guthrum reaches Gloucester and makes camp for the winter.

Exhausted, Alfred goes to his palace at Chippenham, to celebrate Christmas with his family.

Chippenham: 878

EDWARD THREW DOWN his wooden sword and crossed his arms, hugging himself against the cold.

"Why do I always have to be the Danes?" he objected. "It's not fair. I want to be the one who wins sometimes."

"It's because I'm the oldest," explained Fleda. "So I have to be the king of Wessex. I have to be Father."

"But you can't be a king," pointed out Edward, watching the breath curl out of his mouth in a small white cloud. "You're a girl."

Fleda sighed. Boys could be so stupid. "For one thing, we're just pretending. So that means I can be anything I like. And for another, why shouldn't I be a king?" she said, brandishing her sword. "I'd be a very good king. I'd win *all* the time."

They stood silently for a minute, thinking about that.

"We're not winning though," said Edward, not looking at her, "are we?"

Fleda let her sword-arm drop. Her brother looked

very small and very cold. She put her arm round him and hugged him.

"We will win," she promised. "You'll see. In the spring, Father will have them on the run. He'll drive them into the sea. They'll get to the cliffs, and then there'll be nowhere to go, and they'll fall over the edge like so many stones – thump, thump, thump!"

She stamped her foot, once for each thump, and Edward joined in, saying excitedly, "Yes, and they'll smash, won't they, Fleda?"

"Well," said Fleda fairly, "they might not actually smash. Stones don't, usually." Then she brightened. "But the sea washes them away. Yes, that's what will happen – the sea will wash them all away, every last one of them, back to Denmark where they came from!"

She felt something cold and soft touch her cheek like an icy kiss, and she looked up. "Edward – snow!"

At first just a few flakes drifted down, but before long the darkening sky was full of them, whirling and swirling, light and insubstantial. The children gazed at the snow, entranced. Then the door of the hall opened. Golden light spilled out, together with a smell of spicy meat cooking. Fleda's nose twitched.

"Come on, Edward," she said. "Let's go in."

It would be Twelfth Night tomorrow, and the hall was still hung with bunches of holly and mistletoe and garlands of ivy from Christmas. Torches burned, and the huge fire crackled and leaped. But it was strangely quiet,

Fleda thought; it wasn't as it should be. The year before, there had been dancing and songs and storytelling and laughter, lots of laughter and merriment. There was none of that now.

Impatiently, Fleda looked round for her father. He was sitting at the high table, talking with his counsellors and her mother. She took Edward's hand and they ran to tell their parents of the magic outside.

"Father – it's snowing!" she burst out.

"It is!" added Edward excitedly. "It's snowing really fast! They won't come now, will they? No one will come in the snow!"

Ealswith, their mother, drew Edward to her and kissed his snow-spangled brown curls. "Of course not," she murmured. "They're hiding away in Gloucester, miles away from here across the hills. And anyway, no one fights at Christmas-time. We are safe here."

But Fleda was watching her father, waiting to hear what he would say. He gazed past them, as if he could see beyond the walls of the royal palace and through the veils of darkness outside. He was very still, as if every nerve was watching and listening, straining to reach across the cold winter wastes and find out his treacherous enemies, know their thoughts, their plans, their every move. His smoke-blue eyes looked grey and cold, like pieces of flint. His face was like something carved out of stone, stern and bleak.

Fleda shivered. "Father?" she faltered. "That's true, isn't it?"

The room held its breath. Then Alfred turned to her and smiled. His face became her beloved father's face again, relaxed and glowing in the light of the fire.

"Of course it's true. I'll keep you safe, and I'll tell you how. I'll wrap you in a blanket of snow and roll you down the nearest hill, one after the other!" He seized Edward and tickled him till he was helpless with laughter. Then he turned to everyone in the hall and spread his arms out to them, grinning broadly. "Come! We have food, we have ale, and the Christmas season is still with us – let us feast!"

Everyone seemed to relax and the talk and the laughter began. But Fleda watched her father closely, and she saw that the shadows were still there behind his eyes.

Her father had said he would keep them safe and Fleda wanted to believe him. He was the king of Wessex, and he was what stood between them and the fierce, marauding, murderous might of the Danish army. He was their shield, their protection.

It *was* going to be all right. Wasn't it?

Guthrum called a halt. His men would march for as long as he asked them to, he knew that, but he needed all their strength for tomorrow. Alfred had stood in his way for long enough. It was time to put an end to it.

Absently, Guthrum patted the rough warm fur of his horse's neck, and it snickered in appreciation. He looked down the valley. Yes, there it was, just as the scouts had told him it would be – their shelter for

82

the night, a large farm with plenty of outbuildings. It would be a cold night, the coldest of the winter. Not one to be out in the open. Though he himself felt warm enough, with the wolfskin cloak round his huge shoulders and the leather-lined helmet on his head. The snow was falling more thickly now, clustering on his eyebrows and beard.

"Ivar," he growled. "See that farm? We'll rest there. No doubt they've prepared a fine welcome for us!" There was appreciative laughter. "Go down and tell them to leave. Nicely, mind."

"And if they refuse, my lord?" said Ivar, enjoying the joke.

Guthrum smiled. "Then kill them."

Ivar picked his men. He would only need a few. They slipped through the thickening blizzard like wolves. Guthrum waited patiently, listening. When the screams stopped, it would be time to go down.

He hoped the farm was a prosperous one, and that the woman had been a good cook. He was looking forward to his meal.

They came from the sea in swift sleek boats with prows carved in the likeness of dragons, fierce and frightening. But the boats were not as terrible as the men who poured out of them, tall like giants, the wind whipping their long yellow hair and carrying the sound of their shouts towards the people cowering in the monasteries and villages and farms.

Fleda heard their laughter as their huge battleaxes swung through the air and sliced into flesh. She heard the cries of terrified men, women and children as they were dragged from their hiding places, she smelled the blood and the burning and the death, and she searched desperately for the only one who could help: she had to find him before the Danes found her.

But he wasn't there. Try as she might, she couldn't find him. Her father wasn't in any of the places she could think of. He wasn't anywhere. Her heart was hammering, her legs were weak and she couldn't get her breath. There was nowhere left to hide and soon, any minute now—

"Fleda! Hush now, hush! It's a dream, only a dream, you're safe…"

Fleda burrowed blindly into her mother's arms, trying to smother the shaking and the terror in her familiar scent and warmth. Her mother stroked her hair, murmuring soft endearments and gentle words of comfort. At last, Fleda's breathing returned to normal. She could take in the familiar glow of the fire, hear the little sounds people make when they sleep, rustling as they turn over, snoring or just breathing evenly. She was safe. She was in her father's palace at Chippenham, not cowering terrified in a hut by the sea.

"It was so real," she whispered, "and I was looking for Father, but I couldn't find him."

"Shh," murmured Ealswith. "He's here, and we're all safe."

Fleda's eyes began to feel heavy. It was such a relief when the dream ended and she knew for certain that that was all it was, no more than a dream. And it never came more than once in a night. She could let herself sink back into sleep again now.

But not for long. She was suddenly awake again, and this time it was no dream. It was still black dark, and yet someone was pounding on the door, which was unheard of, for this was the king's house. There was urgency and panic in the sound, and for a moment she almost forgot to breathe. Then people were moving in the great hall, and torches must have been hurriedly lit, for she could see light flickering round the edge of the door of the chamber she shared with Edward.

"Fleda?" called Edward. He hadn't woken up earlier, when she'd cried out in her sleep, but was now sitting up and rubbing his eyes. "What's all that noise? What's happening, Fleda?"

She slipped out of bed. "Sshh," she said. "I don't know. I'll find out." The icy night air made her gasp, and she wrapped herself in a thick shawl, hugging it tightly to her for comfort and warmth. She pulled the door open a little way, very quietly.

The king was standing in the centre of the hall. In front of him, in a heap on the floor, was a man, snow mottling his cloak, sparkling like stars as it melted. His head was bent, so Fleda couldn't see his face, only his tangled, dark honey-coloured hair. Two of her father's men were standing by him, one on either side, spears at the ready. Their expressions were grim, and Fleda couldn't tell if the visitor was kneeling by choice, had collapsed in exhaustion, or had been forced down.

She moved closer. The light from the torches didn't reach the shadows at the edges of the hall, and anyway, the men were watching the intruder with the concentrated gaze of a hawk sizing up its prey. They would not notice her. Fleda shivered, and not just with the cold. These men were friends: they often played with her and Edward and her little sisters. Kindly Oswald had carved an ark for them, with animals, two of every kind, and tiny figures of Noah and his wife and sons. Dark, dashing Erluin, with his magic touch with horses, had taught them how to ride, and silver-haired Britnoth had a fund of stories that made their eyes open wide, or in another mood could make them giggle with helpless laughter.

Perhaps it was to do with the way the fitful light from the dying fire and the torches made sharp stones of their eyes and craggy angles of their chins and cheekbones – but Fleda felt suddenly frightened, as if she hardly knew these men. Yet she crept closer, to hear.

Her father leaned forward. He had his cloak round him, and he looked like a great eagle, forbidding and fierce.

"Tell us," he demanded. "Who are you? Why have you come here? What has happened?"

The man's thin shoulders heaved, and his breathing was ragged and harsh. He was quite young, Fleda saw when he looked up; why, he was no more than a boy!

She looked at the men. Did none of them see? He was out of breath – it was like when she ran races with her friends, and tried so hard to win that her breath came in jagged gasps – he *couldn't* speak. She glanced up at the high table, where everyone had sat the night before, eating and laughing and telling stories. It had only been partially cleared, and there were still jugs and cups there. She hurried over, moving silently so that she wouldn't be noticed. The second jug she looked at was still half full of ale, and she poured some of it into a cup. She wrinkled her nose – it smelt disgusting to her, but the grown-ups seemed to like it well enough. Then, carrying it carefully, she brought it over to the group of men beside the fire.

"Drink this," she said firmly to the visitor. "It will help you get your breath."

He looked at her, startled. His mouth was open, but he didn't seem to know what to say. Gratefully, he grasped the cup and drank greedily.

Her father and the other men had turned in surprise when Fleda appeared, and her father was frowning. She smiled apologetically and kneeled down quietly beside his chair. She felt reasonably sure that his need to speak to the visitor would override his concern as to what she was up to, and she was right. With a look – the kind that said he would discuss this with her later – he turned away from her.

"Now then," he said, speaking more gently than

87

before. "You have ridden hard, that's clear to see. Tell us what drove you out on such a night."

The boy lifted his weary head, and began to speak. "The Danes, my lord. They are on the march. They are resting now, at – at my father's farm. They – I think they have killed my family." He fell silent, and his eyes looked beyond them all, into some dark and terrible place that only he could see. "I couldn't help them," he whispered. "They were screaming, and I couldn't help. I wanted to, but – I'd gone out to see to the cattle. They were restless, and Father sent me out to see what was wrong, to quieten them. He always says I have a way with animals, better than him. I was at the doorway of the barn, and suddenly there was this great rushing sound, like thunder and wind – and I heard shouts. Perhaps the snow had muffled the horses' hooves, and that's why I hadn't heard them before. I watched from inside the barn – they smashed down the door with their axes – and then the screaming started. I heard my sister…"

He buried his face in his hands, and then looked up, directly at Alfred. Fleda could see terrible things lurking in his eyes: despair and horror and shame. When he spoke again, he sounded as if he was arguing, pleading, even though no one had said anything.

"I wanted to help – I wanted to save them, but there was nothing I could do – nothing! I was useless, completely useless … there were so many soldiers, and I had no weapon, not even a knife with me." He covered his eyes and went on. His voice sounded dull and lost now. "I waited there in the barn. It wasn't all that long till the screaming stopped, I suppose, but it seemed like for ever. Then more of them rode down – more and more – I've never seen so many men and horses. One of them was the leader – they all looked to him for orders. He was big, like a bear, with long yellow hair. I couldn't see his face. I heard one of the others say that they had cleared out the burrow, that the table was ready for his inspection. He laughed. And then he held up his sword, and shouted, 'Sleep well, Alfred! It'll be the last night that you do!'"

He raised his eyes again. "And that was when I thought of coming here to you. I thought, the king will know what to do. I waited till everything outside seemed quiet. I didn't think they'd left any guards. I couldn't see anyone, and after all, why would they bother? It was only a farm. There was no one who could stop them. I went to the stable. Our horse, Hror, was restless – of course he was. But I quietened him and led him up out of the valley away from the farm, and we rode. It was snowing and bitter but Hror just stretched out his neck and galloped. I think he knew … but in the end, he just couldn't do it any more, his knees gave way. We were almost here, but I had to leave him behind. He was exhausted…" His voice trailed away. He gulped, and went on, "And then I ran the rest of the way. They are coming, my lord. The Danes are coming. They will not be far behind me."

He looked completely, utterly, weary. Fleda bit her lip and looked anxiously at her father. Alfred rose from his chair, grasped the boy's shoulders and pulled him upright. He was tall, Fleda saw, almost as tall as her father.

"Look at me," he said firmly. "What is your name?"

"Ulric," whispered the boy.

"Listen to me, Ulric. You have done well. You have done the best you could possibly do, and that was more than good enough. You could not have saved your family. Nobody could have done that alone. You are in my service now, and I am proud to have you. By riding here as you did, you have saved us and – who knows? – you may even have saved Wessex."

At some point Ealswith had appeared, and now she came forward and put an arm across Ulric's shoulder.

"Come," she said quietly. "You must rest."

Fleda waited eagerly. Now her father would tell them what he was going to do. Oswald, Erluin, Britnoth and the others all leant forward expectantly. Alfred stood up. He walked over to the fire, gazing into the flickering flames. His back was to them. He didn't speak, and the men glanced at each other uncertainly. Fleda watched her father. There was something unfamiliar, worrying, in the line of his shoulders. His head was bowed, and his arms were crossed tightly in front of him. His clenched fists were tucked into his armpits, and she could see his knuckles, with the skin stretched white across them. Uncertainly, she went over to him, and touched his arm.

"Father?" she asked.

He started, and turned to her. "Fleda? Still here?" He bent down, took her face gently in his hands, and kissed the top of her head. Then, seemingly lost in thought again, he turned back to the fire.

For a moment, everyone was still. And then there was another moment, and another – too many moments, Fleda thought anxiously. The Danes might even now have tired of their feasting and be on their way again to Chippenham. But still Alfred said nothing. Erluin stirred impatiently, and was about to speak, but Britnoth stopped him with a gesture, shaking his head. Britnoth was the oldest of her father's counsellors – Fleda looked at him hopefully. Surely he would know what to say?

"My lord," he said finally to the king. "The time is short."

Alfred turned. His eyes were dull grey pools and his face seemed drained of colour.

"Yes," he said quietly. "Indeed it is. Let us sit round the table, like civilized people, and consider what we should do with it."

He placed his hands carefully on the table in front of him, which still held the remains of last night's feast. Then he turned his hands over so that the palms were upwards, the fingers lightly clenched, and studied them. Fleda was puzzled. What was he looking at? They held nothing but air.

"The truth is," he said, "we can do nothing."

Fleda gasped. Was that it? She had been sure he would come up with a plan. How could he possibly speak of doing nothing? There was an unpleasant churning sensation inside her chest, and she recognized it. She knew this fear from her dreams.

Erluin spoke. His dark eyes flashed and he jumped up.

"My lord, surely there must be a way! What if...?" He paused to think, and then went on eagerly. "What if we draw them out away from Chippenham – lure them into a valley – then fall on them!" He smashed a clenched fist into his open hand, and looked hopefully at the king.

Alfred smiled wearily. "How many men do we have here, Erluin?"

Fleda knew – everyone knew – that Alfred's army was a summer one. In the winter, the men went home to look after their families and farms. It was fight enough to survive in the long dark months, when the earth slept, and the cold prowled outside people's houses like a hungry wolf, looking for a way in.

Erluin began to count on his fingers, murmuring names as he went. He got to the end of his right hand, and started again on the left one. Then he stopped, and frowned.

"You see?" said Alfred. "We are only a handful, while Guthrum has a whole army. We could do what you suggest, if there was a suitable valley – which there isn't –

but Guthrum would still win. How could he not?" He sat back in his chair. "I've failed my people," he said quietly. "I've let you all down. Guthrum has broken every promise he's ever made. He lied at Wareham: he killed his hostages, for heaven's sake! Why did I believe him at Exeter?"

"He swore on the bones of a saint!" said Britnoth indignantly. "A sacred oath! He swore a truce – why would you not expect him to keep his word?"

"But our God is not his," pointed out Alfred. "Guthrum walks in darkness. I should have known that the oath would not bind him."

He sank into silence again. The fire was burning low, and it was cold in the great hall.

Britnoth leant forward. "My lord. What is your will? What shall we do?"

Alfred stood up. "For the time being, we must run. But Britnoth, old friend – my family must be safe. I give them into your charge. You must take two thirds of the men, and ride with the Lady Ealswith and my children to Winchester."

Winchester, the capital of Wessex, lay to the south-east.

"They'll be safe with me," said Britnoth gruffly. "I'll protect them with my life – you know that. But you, my lord? What will you do?"

"I'm the one Guthrum wants," said Alfred quietly. "He'll come after me. I will be the bait, the lure. You will leave first, swiftly and secretly, with most of the household. The snow will cover your tracks. The rest of us will go later, when dawn breaks. There will be few of us, and we will take the swiftest horses. We'll make no secret of our going, nor of our direction. When Guthrum arrives in Chippenham, there will be those who'll tell him what he wants to know. He'll follow. But he won't find me."

Ealswith had returned. Her eyes were snapping fire as she listened. She was about to speak, but Alfred put a finger to her lips.

"I will send you word. But if you don't hear – if it becomes necessary, you must take the children overseas to Francia and seek shelter there."

"But—"

"There is no time to argue," he said firmly. "You're safer without me."

"But you, my lord – where will you go?" asked Britnoth.

"A place I know," said Alfred, "a secret place."

Ealswith stared at him. "Where?" she said.

"It's better you don't know," he said. "Secrets shared are easily lost."

Ealswith looked hurt, but his face was closed and he said nothing more. With an impatient gesture of her hands, she hurried off to wake the children. Alfred turned to the others. "Erluin, Oswald – the horses. And food…"

Suddenly, everyone was rushing about, and they all

seemed to have forgotten about Fleda. But that was all right, because she had a plan of her own.

Edward and the little ones, Aethelgifu and Aethelfrith, should be taken to a place of safety. That was as it should be. They were babies. But she was her father's daughter and his oldest child. She would not be left behind. He was flying from danger into danger, but he would not go alone. She would go with him – whether he liked it or not.

But just in case he didn't, she wasn't planning to ask him.

She found her mother with her sisters and their nurse-maid. The children were crying, and clothes were scattered around the room.

"Fleda, where have you been?" said her mother distractedly. "Go and wake Edward – and HURRY!"

Edward had long since grown tired of waiting for Fleda to come back and tell him what was happening; he had curled up and gone back to sleep again. Impatiently, she shook his shoulder.

"Edward, come *on*! You've got to get up and get dressed – NOW! You're going on a journey!"

He sat up, rubbing his eyes. "What? Why? It's the middle of the night," he grumbled. "Are you sure, Fleda? Where are we going?"

"To Winchester," she said briskly. "You like it there, don't you? It's where Sebbi lives." Sebbi was the son of

95

the steward at Winchester, and he and Edward were good friends.

Edward's face brightened, and he jumped out of bed and began pulling on the clothes that Fleda was pulling out of the chest.

"We made a dam last summer, in that little stream that runs into the river. You didn't see it, Fleda, because we didn't let you – it was a secret. And Sebbi's father promised he'd show me how to catch trout – but I suppose it's a bit cold for that now. Where do fish go in the winter, Fleda? Fleda…?" He stared at her, looking puzzled. "Fleda – what are you doing? Why are you putting my trousers on? And that's my new tunic!"

"Yes, yes, I know. But it's too big for you – you said so."

"Yes, but all the same – why have *you* got it on?"

"Because it's warmer than anything I've got. You don't want me to be cold, do you?"

"No, but—"

"Well then. Oh, Edward, do *hurry*!"

"Why? Why do we have to leave in the middle of the night, Fleda? I won't move till you tell me!" He folded his arms and glared at her mutinously. She took a deep breath. She didn't want to frighten him, but he had to know sooner or later.

"That noise we heard earlier, Edward – it was someone who came to warn us. The Danes are coming. And so it's better to go to Winchester, because it's much, much safer there."

His eyes widened in alarm. "What's going to happen? Will Father fight them?"

"No. No, not this time. It'll be perfectly all right – but you must hurry! When you're dressed, go to Mother – she's with the little ones. Tell her – tell her I'm with Britnoth, helping to get the horses ready." She hesitated. His face had turned pale, and fear was stirring in his eyes. She hugged him. "Don't worry. You know Father. Doesn't he always know what to do?"

After he'd gone, she put on a short, fur-lined cloak. It had a hood, and would hide her face. All she had to do was make sure she didn't go to Winchester. She would tell her mother she was riding with Britnoth, and she'd tell Britnoth there'd been a change of plan and she was to ride with her mother. In the dark and the snow and the panic, it would be easy. She'd loiter in the background, unnoticed in her boy's clothing, till Alfred was about to go; and then it would be too late. Her father would have no choice but to take her with him.

Hunched on his horse, Guthrum looked round slowly. He looked as if he was sniffing the air, trying to get a scent of his prey. His men were searching Chippenham, hacking their way into every house, every outbuilding, and into that pathetic church where the Saxons thought their milksop god lived. He heard a cry every now and then as they found someone.

But they wouldn't find Alfred. He'd gone. Guthrum knew it. He'd sensed it as soon as they'd ridden triumphantly up to the doors of

Alfred's palace, only to see them half open, with no smoke issuing from the roof and no sign of life.

Ragnar and Thorkil returned, half dragging a man between them. His feet scuffed a trail in the snow. One of his eyes was bruised, and a thin trail of blood leaked from his nose.

"Who's this?" said Guthrum shortly.

"The smith," said Ragnar cheerfully. "He didn't want to come, but we persuaded him."

Guthrum regarded the man bleakly. "Smiths are useful. We keep smiths. In fact –" he leant forward and bared his teeth in a cold smile – "we reward them if they work for us. Tell me, smith. Where did Alfred go? When did he go?"

The man glared at him. "I saw nothing."

Guthrum drew out his knife and fingered the cutting edge. "A fine piece of work, this. Steel. I'd be interested in your professional opinion." Thoughtfully, he levelled the point in the direction of the smith's eyes. "Be careful, smith, or this may be the last thing you see. Think again. I would, if I were you."

The smith stared at the blade and swallowed. "I – I heard horses. Just after daybreak. He rode east. He's long gone now."

Guthrum nodded, resigned. "He knew. Still, he's left his palace behind. Well stocked with supplies for the winter, I trust." He looked back at the smith. "So your king's gone, smith. Run away with his tail between his legs. What kind of a king is that? Still, no need to worry – you've got a new one now. Spread the word!"

Losing interest in the man, he urged his horse forward. He pushed the door back and rode into the hall. The remnants of last night's feast were still on the table. Guthrum slid off his horse and walked over to the fireplace. He stirred the ashes with his toe. No smoke rose up.

"You're finished, Alfred," he said softly. "You're gone, and so's Wessex. It's all ours. Ours to take, like the rest of this island. Ours to keep." He bent down, picked up some of the ash, and let it sift between his fingers.

"Dust in the wind, Alfred. Dust in the wind. You and all your dreams."

Flight

FLEDA WAS COLD AND EXHAUSTED. She had never been on horseback for this long before. Every bit of her hurt, especially her arms, which felt as if they were being pulled out of their sockets from clinging onto her father. Half her face was buried in his back, but the other half was stinging from the snow. It had stopped for a while just after they'd left Chippenham, but then it had started again – with a vengeance. It no longer felt soft and delicious on her skin, as it had done all that time ago last night when she'd been playing with Edward; now it had turned into vicious little pinpricks of ice which stabbed her skin and hurt so much that she felt like crying.

But she wouldn't cry. She wouldn't make a sound. She wouldn't be a nuisance. Her father had been furious when he'd discovered what she'd done. She didn't want to make him any more cross with her than he already was.

The countryside looked different in the snow. In the forest, the trees looked beautiful, black and white and glistening with crystals. Out in the open, the downs were sculpted into glittering white curves. But once the snow had started again, it was too hard to keep her eyes open; she just wanted to hide as much of her face as she could, and so she tucked it into the rough wool of her father's back. The horse's hooves beat a steady rhythm, and her head nodded in time to it … she was sleepy, and soon she dozed.

When she awoke, the snow had stopped again, and veils of wispy dark cloud were flung out against a sky that flared with bands of gold and orange and scarlet. Oddly, the ground seemed at first to be the same colour as the sky, till she blinked and realized that she was in fact looking at a great sheet of water.

"Is it the sea?" she asked eagerly.

Alfred smiled, and her heart jumped: perhaps he'd forgotten about being angry.

"No, it's not the sea. Look, there are no waves. And I don't think there are trees in the sea – do you?"

It was true. Treetops stood out above the water, and the surface bristled with spiky dark patches, which she supposed must be reeds.

"This is the summer country," explained Alfred. "Somerset. In the summer, it's land. But it's very low lying, and in the winter, it floods and the hills turn into islands. Mostly you need a boat, but there are a few ways through on foot. And I know them."

"How?" she asked curiously.

"I spent a lot of time here as a boy. There's a house – a hunting lodge – near by. I often went there with my father and brothers. It's a good place to hide, and for the time being that's what I must do."

Alfred looked up towards the setting sun and fell silent. Then he turned to the others.

"We must lead the horses. Follow carefully in my steps – unless you want to swim!"

Then he spoke softly to his horse and led him straight out into the water – or so it seemed in the gathering dark. Fleda gasped, and her father laughed.

"Don't worry. It's a causeway. At this time of year it's just below the water so you can't see it, but it's there and it's firm. The people who made it did their job well."

Fleda shivered. A bird's lonely call fluted across the water, and trails of pearly mist had begun to drift around their feet. When she looked back, the small line of horses behind her looked as if they were floating. She had the feeling that they were cutting themselves off from all that was familiar, and heading into something strange and unknown.

She was uncertain how long it was before the dark shape of an island reared up before them and, thankfully, the horses stepped onto dry land.

"Here it is," said Alfred, looking round – though between mist and darkness there was little to see.

"Athelney. The Island of the Princes. My land!"

But Fleda wondered. This place was wild and lonely. It didn't feel to her as if it belonged to anyone.

Athelney: January 878

FLEDA'S FATHER HAD MANY HOUSES, and they moved from one to another according to need and the season. At the end of every journey she'd made till now, there had been a hall lit by torches and the cheerful, gently flickering light of a great fire. There had been a bed, with warm coverings and sheepskins to sleep on, and there had been clean, sweet smelling rushes on the floor. There had been food and a warm welcome for the lord of every hall, the king of Wessex and his family.

In Athelney, there was no welcome. Their destination was a hunting lodge that had not been used for many years. There was no light, no fire. But they could see a collection of thatched buildings on top of the long, low hill which rose up out of the marshes, and Alfred led his small party to the largest of them. A little daylight lingered, but when Fleda peered through the doorway, she could see only shadows. She heard small scurrying sounds, and she flinched as something ran over her foot.

But the roof turned out to be sound, the floor was dry, and plenty of wood was stacked up against the walls outside, under the shelter of the overhanging thatch.

Soon, they had a fire crackling merrily in the hearth. Ulric, looking glad to be busy, had found a broom and swept the floor clean. Fleda smiled to see him and asked if there was anything she could do. He looked doubtful for a moment, and she could see that he was thinking that she was a princess and this surely wasn't the kind of thing princesses did, but she raised an eyebrow and said that there must be something she could do to help, and he smiled shyly and took her with him to look for blankets and see if they could find any food.

They found blankets and sheepskins folded away in chests with dried herbs to keep them sweet, and spread them out round the fire to drive away the tinge of damp that had crept into them despite all the care someone had taken.

There was a barrel of weak ale, and a side of bacon wrapped in cloth hanging from the rafters, and some onions and barley, and from these things Ulric made a sort of broth. Fleda was full of admiration. She knew nothing of cooking: there were normally servants to do that kind of thing. She told Ulric it was the best soup she'd ever tasted, and he blushed.

She was tired to the bone from the long ride and the early start, and soon her weariness and the heat from the fire turned everything into a pleasant blur, and her eyelids grew heavy. She could hear the men talking quietly. She waited till she'd made sure her father's voice was among them, and then she let herself sink into a deep, comforting sleep.

Next morning when she woke, it was a puzzle at first to work out where she was. She sat up, rubbing the sleep out of her eyes, and looked round. She was on one of the sleeping benches which ran all the way round the room. At first she thought she was alone, but then she saw Oswald. He was stoking the fire with logs. She stretched and yawned.

"At last!" said Oswald cheerfully, looking round. "Come and have some breakfast. It's not much, but soon we should be better supplied. Erluin and Eadric have gone to the nearest village to see what they can find, and Ricbert's gone fishing with Ulric. Useful lad, that. I don't think they'll have much luck though."

"Why?" asked Fleda.

"Come and see," grinned Oswald.

Outside, Fleda gasped. It all looked very different from the night before. The sun shone down brightly from a periwinkle blue sky, and lit up a landscape made of sheets of glittering ice, edged by lines of trees and speckled with clumps of marsh grass and reeds, which made sharply cut patterns against the silver and white.

"Oh!" said Fleda, enchanted.

"Yes, it's pretty, isn't it? But I think all the fish will stay nice and snug under the ice – don't you? I don't see how Ulric and Ricbert will manage to get at them. Still, we'll see. Maybe Ulric has a trick or two up his sleeve. He seems a handy kind of lad."

They went back inside. The bread was several days old now, and hard and dry, but Oswald stuck it on the point of his knife and held it close to the fire till it was toasted. Then, with a flourish, he produced some honey that he'd found.

"It's all gold!" said Fleda in delight. "Gold bread and golden honey."

"A feast fit for a princess," said Oswald, bowing. Then he looked at her and his mouth twitched. Puzzled, she glanced down at herself, and saw that she was still wearing Edward's trousers and tunic. She burst out laughing.

She bit hungrily into the honey-soaked toast, ate another piece as well and licked her fingers clean. Then she looked directly at Oswald.

"What are we going to do now?" she said.

Oswald thought for a minute. "Well, we could have a good look round outside and see what's what and what's where. That would be useful, wouldn't it? It's an old place, this – been around for a good few years. Who knows what we might find!"

This sounded interesting, but it wasn't what Fleda had meant.

"No, no – I mean, what are we going to do next? We can't just stay here, can we? So what's going to happen?"

Oswald threw some more wood on the fire.

"Well now, I'm not exactly sure, to tell the truth. For the moment, we just have to lie low here." He looked at her seriously. "No one must know who we are – who your father is. This is a secret place, a hidden place. It's very difficult to find, even when you know it's there, so it should be very safe. But if Guthrum was to get an inkling where your father is, he'd find someone to show him the way. We'd fight to the death, but there aren't enough of us to protect him against an army."

Suddenly, Fleda realized that she didn't know where her father was, and she asked Oswald.

"He's gone out into the marshes. Don't worry," he said hastily, seeing her worried look, "he knows the paths, he knows where it's safe to go. We hunted here a lot when we were boys. I offered to go with him, but ... he wants some peace and quiet, for thinking. He does that a lot. Too much, I sometimes think."

They went outside to investigate the island. Oswald was puzzled. "Someone's been looking after it," he said. "Everything's in good order. And there was the food, and the beer. And yet no one's living here. Perhaps they just use it in the summer, when the floods go down. The grazing must be good then."

While he looked round the outbuildings, Fleda went down towards the water's edge. The ice fascinated her. She tapped it with her foot, gingerly at first, and then harder. It was solid, even at the edge, and it would probably be even thicker further out. She wished she had her skates. All the children had a pair, carved by Oswald out of bone. Perhaps he would be able to make her some more. She looked round to see where he was so that she could ask him. He was coming down the hill towards her, stepping carefully so as not to slip.

As she turned back again, she thought she saw something out of the corner of her eye – something dark, close to a line of willows. She shaded her eyes with her hand; she was looking almost into the sun, and the glitter on the ice was dazzling.

"See something?" asked Oswald.

"I thought I did," she said, still squinting. "I thought there was something – someone – over there, by those trees."

Oswald became very still, and followed the direction of her gaze. Then he relaxed. "Most probably just the shadow of a bird, reflected in the ice. It's difficult to see, with the sun low down like it is. Or maybe it was a fox, or a deer, even."

"Or Father," she suggested. "Perhaps it was Father on his way back."

"Yes – it could have been," he agreed.

They stood looking for a little longer, and then Fleda noticed a hill in the distance. It rose straight up out of the flat land. It was bare of trees, its outline stark against the sky. On top of it was a tower.

"What's that?" she said curiously.

"It's Glastonbury Tor. There's an abbey there, at the bottom of the hill."

"What's that tower on top of it? Is it part of the abbey?"

"I don't know," said Oswald. "Perhaps it's another church. There's something strange about that hill. Wherever you go in these parts, you can see it, as if it's at the centre of everything..."

Suddenly they heard voices, and Ulric and Ricbert appeared from the other side of the island.

"Look at the teeth on this pike!" said Ricbert, grinning and holding up a large fish. "It's a monster."

"I didn't know you knew anything about fishing," said Oswald in disbelief.

"Well, I had a bit of help from young Ulric here. He knew where I should try – and he says he knows how to cook it too!"

They set off back up the hill. Oswald and Ricbert were arguing cheerfully, and so it was natural for Ulric to fall behind and walk with Fleda. He had long legs, and she had to hurry to keep up with him. She stole a glance at him. How dreadful it must be to have lost his family – if he had, of course. Then a thought struck her. Could he be absolutely sure that they'd died?

"Perhaps – perhaps your family weren't all killed," she said impulsively. "I mean, Guthrum didn't need to kill them, did he?"

He stopped and stared at her in astonishment. The

laughter had drained away from his face, and she suddenly wished she hadn't said anything.

"Of course he didn't need to," he said. "He doesn't need a reason to kill, does he? He was enjoying it. They were nothing to him – nothing!"

"I'm sorry," she said feebly. He didn't seem to hear her.

"He'll pay," he said slowly. "One day, he'll pay. Your father will meet him on the battlefield, and I'll be there. I'll watch him die. I hope it's slow, and I hope it's painful."

There was silence for a moment, and then Fleda made an excuse and went after the others. She was almost stumbling in her haste to be away from him. Her father had taken part in many battles – so had all of them. But she had never been there. She'd heard about the Danes – they strode through her nightmares – but she'd never actually seen them, never seen close up the evidence of what they did. But she'd seen it just now, in the horror lurking behind Ulric's eyes. And she didn't want to face it.

When Freda arrived back at the house, Alfred was there before her, gazing absently into the fire. She threw her arms round him and buried her face in his chest, and he smiled and stroked her hair.

"There, my little one," he murmured in surprise. "What's this?"

She shook her head, and he sighed. "You shouldn't be here. It's no place for a child. Erluin was to see if he could find a woman, someone to look after you. They'll be back

111

soon, he and Eadric – perhaps they'll have news for us."

She sat back. "I don't need to be looked after," she objected. "And even if I did, Oswald looks after me. And you do too."

Before he could answer, the door was flung open, and Erluin and Eadric came in, stamping their feet and slapping their hands.

"Getting cold again," growled Eadric. His stubby nose was red, and his feet and legs were wet.

"You really shouldn't have gone for a paddle," said Erluin, grinning. "It can't have helped."

"It didn't," answered Eadric. "And it wasn't intentional. It's not easy to stay out of the water round here, is it? Did you notice the people in Aller had a funny way of walking? Webbed feet, mark my words – just like ducks'."

He pulled off his boots and held a foot up to the fire, inspecting gloomily the cloud of steam that rose from it.

"So tell us," said Alfred. "What news?"

"None about the Danes, as you'd imagine," said Eadric. "I shouldn't think news travels fast down here. Well, not unless it has wings or fins. Or webbed feet, of course. And we couldn't ask too much, or say too much – we didn't want to give away your presence, my lord. We told them we were just a band of soldiers sent by the king to protect his interests in this area – and particularly to protect them. They liked that bit, couldn't do enough for us after that. Though the reeve didn't have much to say, I did notice that: he kept his own counsel and let

112

others do the talking for the most part."

"He watched everything, though," added Erluin, "and he listened."

"Yes. And he did say that he knew of someone who might come and look after us," said Eadric, with a glance at Fleda. "A woman called Cerys."

"Cerys?" Alfred looked up sharply. "Did you say Cerys?"

"Yes, my lord. It's an odd name, isn't it?" The reeve said that she lives in this house in the summer, and grazes her animals on Athelney. It's she who's taken care of the place, kept it up together."

Erluin was looking impatient with these domestic details. "My lord," he said, "I thought – we thought – that perhaps we should take the reeve into our confidence. We need more men, and he should be able to help."

Alfred looked at him, but in a vague sort of way, as if he couldn't quite focus.

"Do we? To do what?"

Erluin frowned, puzzled. "Why – to fight back against Guthrum, my lord."

"And do you really suppose we could take on the whole of the Great Heathen Host with the aid of a few peasants?" The king's voice was bleak and despairing.

They all stared at him in shocked silence. Oswald was the first to speak.

"My lord," he said hastily, "you're not yourself. Perhaps you should rest."

Alfred shivered. "Yes, perhaps I should ... is it cold in here? I can't seem to get warm."

Ulric jumped up and threw another log onto the fire. The room was already very warm: it wasn't large – tiny, compared to the halls at Chippenham and Winchester – and the fire was banked high. Fleda noticed that her father was pale except for his cheeks. They were red – too red, feverishly red. He sneezed.

"Father?"

"It's nothing," he said. "Just a chill."

The shivering didn't stop and, before nightfall, Alfred took himself off to bed, saying that a good night's sleep would soon sort him out. But by the next day, he had developed a painful cough, which racked him, leaving him shuddering and exhausted. His skin was hot to the touch. Fleda melted ice, and soaked cloths in the cold water and bathed his forehead. For a little while, he would sigh and look more peaceful, but soon he would be tossing and turning again, plucking at his covers and murmuring words that they couldn't properly hear.

Fleda came out of his room in despair. Her mother knew how to care for the sick – how to make them comfortable, which herbs to use to bring down a temperature or ease aches and pains – but Fleda didn't have her mother's skill.

"We must get help," she said to Oswald with a stricken look. "We must find someone who knows what to do.

114

He's really ill, and I can't – I don't know how to nurse him."

Suddenly, the fire seemed to dim down, and then just as quickly it flared up again with a brilliant emerald and violet light. Startled, they were both looking at it when a voice came from behind them, a soft, lilting voice.

"I am Cerys. I think you knew that I might come?"

They whirled round. A woman stood in the doorway. She had a long fall of gleaming dark hair and eyes of so pale a blue they were almost silver. She smiled, particularly at Fleda, who for some reason felt immediately relieved. She went over to Cerys, though Oswald looked uneasy and made a motion with his hand as if to stop her.

"My father is ill," she said simply. "Can you help him?"

Fleda took Cerys to see Alfred. She laid her cool hand on his head, and her touch seemed to calm him. Then she asked Fleda to heat some water and bring it to her in a cup. She added some dried herbs, which she took from linen sachets she had in a pouch tied to her belt. She and Fleda helped Alfred to sit up, just enough for him to sip the infusion from the cup.

There was a candle burning on a ledge above Alfred's bed. Cerys produced a small flagon, again from the pouch, and poured a few drops onto the wick. The scent of lavender filled the room. She gave Fleda a tranquil smile.

"First he will dream," she said, "and then he will rest."

The Dark Time

A LFRED DREAMED.

At first, his dreams were turbulent and full of blood and battles, anguished screams and cruel faces – his own included. Part of him knew that there were decisions to be taken and plans to be made, but he had been fighting for so long, and he was tired, so very, very tired. Desperate to escape it all, he allowed himself to sink further and further, deep into gentler dreams.

It was the third day of her father's illness. Fleda was gazing at him, wondering if perhaps he looked a little better, when suddenly he sat up. His eyes were bright and excited, and his cheeks were flushed. But his skin looked dry and stretched, as if it would crackle if you touched it.

He stared at Fleda, looking puzzled, and then his face clouded.

"Oh. It was just a dream, then," he said, sounding sad. "I thought we were going to Rome."

"Rome, Father?"

He reached out and took her hands, and placed them, one on each side of his face. It was burning.

"Ah – that's better!" he said. "You have cool hands, like your mother's."

Then his eyes searched the room. He looked confused. "I thought someone else was here," he said. "A woman. Did I dream that, too?"

Fleda looked round. She hadn't noticed Cerys leaving.

"No," she said gently. "You didn't dream it. Cerys was here. She's been helping me to look after you."

He looked eager. "Cerys? Is it the same Cerys? Has she...?"

"What, Father?"

He frowned, as if he was trying to remember something. "I think I was going to ask if she had forgiven me."

She stared at him. Was he still dreaming?

"I'll fetch you some water," she said. "You should drink as much as you can. Cerys said that."

"Yes," he said. "Then I will."

He drank thirstily, and then he lay down and slept again.

The next time he woke, he seemed quieter and more himself. Fleda took a deep breath. There was something she wanted to know.

"Father," she said. "When did you and Cerys meet? And why would she need to forgive you?"

She helped him to sit up. Ulric had brought the softest sheepskins he could find, and piled them up so that Alfred could rest his head on them. She moved them a little and her father leaned against them. His face was pale, but the hectic red patches on his cheeks had faded and he looked more himself.

"Would you open the door a little?" he asked her. "I'd like to see the daylight."

She did as he asked, and he gazed out. The doorway framed a view of the marshes stretching out towards a nearby hill, similar to Glastonbury but smaller. Trees and undergrowth shadowed the water. It was a secret, mysterious landscape, very different from the chalk hills and clear skies that Fleda was used to.

"My brothers and I often hunted here when I was a child..." began Alfred. "Have I told you that already? I'm sorry – my head feels full of fog. Anyway, as I was saying, I was the youngest, and there were times when I was tired of that and wanted to strike out on my own." He smiled at her. "A little like Edward, perhaps."

That startled Fleda for a moment. At night, when she curled up to go to sleep, and in the mornings when she woke up, she would picture her mother, Edward and the little ones, and she'd wonder what they were doing in Winchester and if they missed her. But mostly she found it was better not to think of them. She listened as Alfred began to tell her a strange story, about a girl with silver eyes and a deer he should not have shot...

"I never forgot Cerys," he ended. "I never spoke of what happened that day, but it remained with me. I knew it meant something, something important, but I've never understood what. I know how I felt, though. I felt ashamed."

Fleda stirred, and he looked at her in surprise. She realized he had been so wrapped up in his story that he'd almost forgotten she was there; it was as if he'd been talking to himself. But now he smiled.

"So that's why I was surprised when you said that Cerys had been looking after me. I don't know why she would. But perhaps I imagined half of it. Or perhaps it's a different Cerys."

"No," said Fleda. "I don't think so. She definitely sounds like the same person. The silver eyes. And – other things."

"Oh." His face clouded. "But she's gone?"

"Yes, I think so. But I expect she'll be back."

The talking had exhausted him, and soon his eyes closed and he was asleep again.

Oswald prowled round the room. He hated being indoors. But even if he went out, there was nowhere to go. He supposed he could walk round the island – again – but then he'd probably bump into the others, and they'd just start arguing once more. He was worried. They all were. They'd fled to Athelney with Alfred because he was their lord and it was their duty and they trusted him. Oswald had been through many battles with Alfred these last ten years, and Alfred had never wavered. He would spend a lot of time thinking – more, Oswald sometimes thought, than was really healthy – but in the end, he would make a decision, and it was nearly always a good one.

But this time, Oswald wasn't sure. He'd thought Alfred must have some plan at the back of his mind, and coming to Athelney was just the first part of it. But now, here they were, in this strange place, cut off and alone, and if there was any plan, Alfred was keeping it very close to his chest … talking of which, on top of everything else, Alfred was ill. His chest had always been weak, but now his breathing was so bad you could hear him wheezing from the next room. This Cerys had certainly eased him, with her herbs and potions, but there was something strange about her. One minute she was there, and the next minute she wasn't. Uncanny, it was – unnerving. These British were all the same: tricky, slippery people. Most of them lived far out on the fringes – in Wales, or distant Cornwall – and just as well, as far as Oswald was concerned. They were no friends of the Saxons, that was for sure, and yet he and the others were depending on Cerys to make the king better.

What if he didn't get better? What would happen to Wessex then? Oswald sighed.

"That's a great sigh, Master Oswald," said a musical, mocking voice close beside him.

She'd done it again! Exasperated, he glared at her.

"Why can't you make a noise when you come into a room, like ordinary people?" he complained. Or there was that thing with the fire that she'd done the first night. Oswald thought it was just a trick, but the others had been awe-struck; they thought she was a witch at the very least, maybe even an enchantress. He decided not to mention it, just in case she was a witch and she took it the wrong way.

"You were deep in thought," said Cerys. "Otherwise, you would have heard me."

He turned away, and stared into the fire. "Well, there's plenty to think about," he said.

"You're afraid for the king," she said.

"I'm afraid for all of us," he said gloomily. Then, with a start, he realized what she'd said. She wasn't supposed to know who Alfred was. He stared at her. "How did you know?" he whispered. "No one was supposed to tell you ... or did Fleda say?"

"She did not. There was no need. It's clear from the way you all honour him that he is a great lord – and besides that, he has not changed so much since he came here as a young prince with his brothers. I recognized him as soon as I saw him. There are others, too, who would remember him. But you need not be afraid. Like myself, they know how to be silent."

She smiled. A little grudgingly, he smiled with her, then asked, "How is he? When will he be well again?"

This time when she spoke, there was no laughter in her voice, no mockery.

"As the year grows stronger, so will he. He will be the king that you need – that we all need – but he is very weak and it will take time. In the meantime, Math, the reeve, wishes to meet you. There are ways he can help. What may I tell him?"

Oswald thought for a moment. What would Alfred want him to do? He wasn't sure. But something needed to happen. The others were getting edgy, impatient – especially Erluin. He was a good lad, but a bit of a hot-head... Oswald made up his mind.

"Tomorrow," he said. "Tell him to come tomorrow. I'll send Ulric to guide him."

The smile again, hardly there and soon gone. "He needs no guide. You are safe here from strangers – they would never find the way to Athelney. But this is our land. We know it. And we will protect it, and those we allow into it."

It didn't seem to matter how much Alfred slept, he was still tired. He had suffered with his chest for many years now, though not, so far as he remembered, when he was a child. When the weakness came on, every breath was a struggle: a fierce, painful effort to draw in air. He knew he could overcome it – he just had to concentrate, to focus all his strength on remaining calm, mastering his body, willing himself to breathe slowly, deeply. Perhaps it was a test, sent by God – after all, what kind of king could he be, if he failed even to master his own body?

This was the crux of it, the thing that truly tormented him. How was he to be the king that Wessex needed? What kind of a king did Wessex need?

Any child could give him the obvious answer to that: Wessex needed a king who could protect its people against the Danes. But how could he do that any longer? He was a fugitive with a handful of men, hiding in the marshes. That being so, how could he possibly conquer an army and make a place that would be safe – a place where children like Fleda and boys like Ulric would not be haunted by memories that were worse than nightmares, or forced to hide for fear of sudden murder?

What if he failed?

He closed his eyes. It would be so much easier to stop thinking, to stop trying. Just to sink into sleep, into restful darkness.

No. He had no intention of doing that.

He could make use of this time. During the days and nights that he'd shivered and sweated with fever, he'd been visited by dreams. Like the memory of Cerys, they seemed to mean something.

There were lessons to be learned; there was a reason for all this. Somehow, he had to discover within himself the strength and the vision to inspire his people and lead them to victory. The clues were in the past. He set himself to find them.

The Northmen had turned the full force of their attention on the Isles of Britain very soon after Alfred was born. His whole life had been lived under their shadow. There had been so many battles, fought first by his father, then by his brothers, then, these last seven years, by Alfred himself. Sometimes he'd won, and hope had dared to stir, like a mouse rustling in dry leaves, but then would come defeat, often stained with treachery, with broken treaties and oaths betrayed, and hope would creep back into the dark again.

For his sake, for his people's sake, he had to find a way to stop this cycle. He knew, through the mists of his weakness, that his men were waiting for him to come to life, to give them direction. Fleda too — he saw the faith in her eyes. She believed in him, and he couldn't bear the thought of disappointing her.

The coughing began again. It started with a scratch at the back of his throat. And then came the tearing pain, as if his chest was being hacked open. Aelle, in the north, and Edmund, in the east, had felt pain worse than this … it was said that the Northmen had performed the rite of the blood eagle on them. It was an act of homage, apparently, to the king of their gods, Odin. Alfred wasn't sure whether he believed it or not, but from what he'd seen of Guthrum, he wouldn't be surprised if it were true. How could you deal with men whose gods had such fearsome appetites?

The spasm over, Alfred closed his eyes for a moment.

Perhaps it hadn't really happened after all. In any case, there was no use thinking about such things.

He had a feeling there was something he was missing. Something he'd lost somewhere along the way. And if he could only find it, he'd know how to deal with the Danes. How to tame them, so there'd be no more broken oaths, no more slaughter in the night, no more anguished cries rising with the smoke from burning villages. Was it his fault? Was God punishing him for something he'd done – or for something he hadn't done?

The next direction he took had to be the right one. All he had to do was find it.

But soon – it must be soon. Everyone was waiting. Fleda, his family in Winchester, his thegns in the neighbouring hut; the whole of Wessex.

Everything rested on him.

Fleda watched her father. His face was pale, but he seemed to be sleeping. She'd hurried in when she'd heard him coughing. Cerys had shown her how to make a drink with honey and mead – it would soothe him, she said. But Fleda didn't think she should disturb him if he'd gone back to sleep.

Then his eyes opened, blue and light, like a summer sky.

"Father?" she said. "Do you feel better?"

He smiled at her, and sipped gratefully at the warm golden liquid.

"I had such a good sleep," he said. "I was dreaming…"

Usually the dreams that disturbed his sleep seemed to be unpleasant; this one must have been different.

"What were you dreaming about?" she asked curiously.

He looked at her thoughtfully. "Would you really like to hear? Would it really interest you?"

"Yes, it would," she said firmly.

She settled herself comfortably at the end of his bed, ready to listen. She hadn't often had him to herself like this, and on this tiny, waterlogged island, there was little enough she could do that was useful. He began to speak.

"I was dreaming about a journey I made when I was a child – younger than you, Fleda. It was the most amazing journey. My father took me to Rome."

He'd mentioned Rome before, she remembered. "What was it like?" she asked. She tried to think of the biggest town she knew of. "Was it as big as Winchester?"

He smiled. "Bigger. Oh, so much bigger. You can't imagine it, Fleda. Any more than I could, when my father told me we were going to go there." He paused. The lines of his face were relaxed, and she could tell that he was no longer seeing the small bare room on the island of Athelney. He was far away and long ago: a small boy, listening to his father.

He talked and talked. He told her about the journey to Rome, about Cerdic and his ship, the *Raven*, about the nights spent in monasteries or, occasionally, under the

126

stars. He told her about the forests and vineyards of Francia, and the astonishing beauty of the snow-capped mountains.

But then he began to cough again, and Fleda was cross with herself. She had been so wrapped up in her father's story that she had forgotten how weak he was. His energy was completely spent, and he lay back, trying to breathe slowly and deeply.

"You must rest, Father," she said, jumping up to pass him his drink and smooth the covers.

After a while, he was able to speak again, though his voice was faint and weak. "There's so much I want to tell you," he whispered. "So much I haven't thought about for a long time. It helps, to talk to you. But I think I will have to sleep now..."

His eyes closed, and Cerys was there beside Fleda again. Once again, she sprinkled something onto the wick of the candle.

"He must sleep deeply," she said. "He needs to rest, so that his body can heal itself."

Fleda looked at Cerys. Her hair had fallen forward, shadowing her face, and Fleda couldn't see her eyes. Suddenly afraid, she clutched Cerys's arm.

"He will get better, won't he?" she demanded.

"I think so," said Cerys, in a strange, tight voice. "I hope so."

They were all worried about the king. He was restless,

and often muttered words that no one could quite hear, but it was some time since he'd woken properly. There was an unhealthy tinge of colour in his cheeks, and the breath rattled in his chest. The weather had turned from sharp crisp cold to a damp, dark chill which seeped into all their bones and refused to be completely driven off by the fire, even though Ulric took anxious care to keep it stacked high.

They had decided that someone should sit with the king through the night, and Fleda insisted on taking her turn. She was vaguely aware that Oswald, Erluin and the others were growing more and more tense. She heard snatches of muttered conversations and arguments, without being able to hear exactly what they were saying, and once Erluin came in, looking angry. He said nothing, but his dark, hawk-like face was brooding and anxious as he watched the king, and she could feel him willing her father to get better.

Her eyes felt itchy and tired now, and she rubbed them as she and Cerys stood looking at Alfred. Absently, Cerys reached out and touched her wrist.

"Don't rub them," she said. "It'll only make them worse."

Fleda felt a jolt of recognition. "That's what my mother always says!"

Cerys smiled. "Well, if we both say so, then perhaps it's true and you should take notice!"

Fleda put her hands behind her back. She felt oddly

comforted for a moment. Then she turned back to her father. His hands plucked restlessly at the covers that Oswald had piled on him to make sure he was warm enough.

"He's worse again, isn't he?" she said sadly. "He's been like that all night. And even when he opens his eyes, I don't think he really sees me."

"Yes," said Cerys, laying her hand on his forehead. "This damp weather does him no good. The fever has come back. We must cool him down." She heaved off some of the covers, and Fleda helped her.

"We need cold water," said Cerys. "I'll fetch some."

Fleda kneeled beside her father. He kept muttering, and she tried to catch the words. Some of them sounded like Latin. She knew a little: her father had always been insistent that his children should learn to read. Her mother had sniffed and said that perhaps she could see the point for Edward, but she certainly couldn't for Fleda – but Alfred had appeared to listen carefully and then found a tutor for them anyway.

"*Gentis Anglorum*," she whispered, "of the English people… What is he thinking about? Where have you gone, Father? Where are you?"

Cerys slipped quietly back into the room. In the flickering light from the fire, she could see the curved line of Fleda's cheek. It glistened. Cerys put down the water and the cloths she was carrying, and put her arm round Fleda's shoulders.

129

"He is ill – very ill," she said fiercely, "but we will make him better. And in the meantime, we must be strong for him, as he will later be strong for all of us. Remember, Fleda, you are a princess. You are your father's daughter, and you have a part to play. Math, the reeve, will come soon to talk with Oswald and the others, and there will be decisions to make. While the king is ill, you must help to make them."

Fleda's eyes widened. "Me? But will they listen?"

"You will make them listen," said Cerys firmly. "Remember who you are! You are the king's daughter, a princess of the House of Wessex, and you have a right to be heard. But for now ... " She wrung out a cloth, folded it, and placed it on Alfred's forehead. "For now, we watch."

It was shaping up to be an uneasy meeting. Oswald and Erluin had decided that they should keep a guard at the far end of the causeway. Ricbert, bored like the rest of them and eager for something to do, had readily volunteered for the job. If the reeve approached, he was to give a special whistle. If a stranger came near, he was to make a sound like an owl.

So they were taken aback when someone hammered on the door and flung it open. Oswald leapt to his feet, his sword suddenly in his hand, but Eadric grabbed his arm.

"No – no, it's the reeve!"

The man in the doorway lifted an eyebrow, and waited.

Oswald scowled. "How did you get here?"

Erluin had his hand on his knife, and he said tersely, "There was a man on guard. What's happened to him?"

Math, the reeve, shrugged. "Watching the water birds. Throwing stones into the water... I wouldn't know. We didn't see him. Where was he?"

"At the end of the causeway," said Oswald.

Math smiled slightly. "That's the way for strangers. There are other paths, if you know where to find them. May I come in?" He stepped inside and looked coolly at Erluin. "If we'd wanted to take you just now, we could have done. Easily. If what Cerys tells us is true, you have reason to be more careful."

Erluin's eyes flashed. He opened his mouth to speak, but Oswald got in first.

"Cerys?" he said, looking exasperated. But before he could say any more, Fleda entered.

"Cerys is with my father," she said.

Math bowed his head to her. He was tall and wiry and dark. Laughter lurked at the corners of his mouth and the back of his pale blue eyes. Fleda wasn't sure whether it was kindly or mocking.

"I am sorry for his illness," he said quietly.

She nodded slightly, and sat down.

Oswald spoke gruffly. "Have you any news? Have you heard anything of Guthrum?"

Math bowed slightly.

"What I have, I will share. Guthrum makes no effort to keep his activities secret. His men go where they will and take what they want. They seize grain from the barns and food from wherever they find it, and they kill those who stand in their way. In fact they kill people whether or not they stand in the way.

"And they are searching. Wherever they go, they ask for the whereabouts of the king. This is what we have heard. And it's not only the Danes who do that; many others are asking the same question."

He paused, and his eyes ranged round the room. Oswald was looking at the ground. Erluin was leaning against the wall, his arms folded, his eyes unfriendly. Eadric's normally open, friendly face was flushed with anger.

"My own question is this," went on Math. "The king of Northumbria is dead. So is the king of East Anglia. Burgred of Mercia has fled overseas. Out of all our mighty leaders, only the king of Wessex remains. He is ill, we know that. But tell me – if he were not ill, what would he be doing? Would he be standing against Guthrum? Or would he do as Burgred did? Would he save himself, and abandon his people?"

Oswald looked up suddenly. Erluin's face flared into anger. Math found himself at the centre of a very unfriendly circle.

But it was Fleda who spoke first, not one of the men.

Inside she was angry, but her voice was cool and polite.

"When my father is better," she said to Math, "he will fight Guthrum. But he can't do it alone. What about you? Where do you stand? Are you with us? Or are you just watching, and waiting to see who wins?"

There was a sharp intake of breath. Fleda didn't look to see who it came from.

Math was silent for a moment, and very still. Then he said, "When he was a boy, your father won himself many friends in these parts.

"But later, he grew more distant from us. We had bad years when the crops failed. There was little to eat. Many died – mostly old people and children. If you had seen the children..." He was silent for a moment. "Help was sought ... it was not forthcoming." Oswald started to say something, but Math held up his hand to stop him. "He and his brother were fighting, it's true. But as much as the people depend on their king, he depends on them. If the king leads us against Guthrum, I will follow. So will we all. But – it must be recognized. We have a duty to the king. But he has a duty to us, too. And he must remember that – not just when he needs us, but always."

"When my father is well," said Fleda, "you will be able to speak of these things with him. But in the meantime, you have offered us your help – " she glanced round, particularly at Oswald – "and I know my father would want to thank you for it, and that he would want you all to work together, to do what needs to be done in readiness for his recovery. Which will come," she said steadily. "You may be sure of that."

She took a deep breath. Was it enough? Would they be able to talk now, instead of just needling each other?

"It seems to me," she said gently, "that there must be things that could be done, even though the king is ill. Things that shouldn't wait. But of course, I don't know much about it." Then she sat down quietly at the edge of the room.

After that, the talking went on for what seemed like hours. They were all jumpy and quick to take offence but, in the end, they managed to agree on a number of things. The first was that Alfred would have to fight Guthrum. The second, was that he would need men to join him.

"How many men?" asked Math.

"More than Guthrum, if possible," said Oswald gloomily.

"And how many men does Guthrum have?" said Math patiently.

"Thousands," said Oswald. "And before you ask," he added, "I don't know exactly how many thousands."

"Does anyone know?" asked Math.

No one answered.

"Then we need to find out," said Erluin. "Math's right. We need to send messages out. All over Wessex. In secret." He turned to Math. "You're the reeve. You must have contacts with other reeves in other shires. Can you help?"

Math nodded. "Of course. But I think the first thing is to get in touch with Aethelnoth."

"Aethelnoth? Who's he?" asked Eadric, his round cheerful face confused as he tried to keep up with what everyone was saying.

Math looked politely surprised. "He's the ealdorman of Somerset. He already has a network in place. He can contact the other reeves in Somerset, and the ealdormen in the other shires.

"The second thing would be to fortify the island," said Math. "It's well hidden, but even so ... all an enemy would need to do would be to find a guide, and then he could just walk in. As I did," he added, looking round quizzically.

The king's men looked a little shamefaced.

"Perhaps it's something for you to think about," said Math placidly. "Of course, I could make one or two suggestions..."

Fleda left then, and went to see how her father was. Cerys had dipped a square of linen in water, and was using it to wipe his face. She answered the question in Fleda's eyes.

"He is quieter," she said, "and a little cooler, I think."

Fleda told her as much as she could remember about what had been said.

"The reeve," she said shyly, "he reminds me a bit of you."

Cerys smiled. "We are of the same people," she said.

Fleda was puzzled. "But – of course you are," she said. "We all are, aren't we?"

Dusk was gathering, and the room was shadowy. Cerys's eyes gleamed silver like the moon.

"Not exactly," she said. "You Saxons have been here a long time. But we were here first. Many us were driven out when your people came. But some of us stayed. We are British, Math and I. And yes – your eyes are sharp. He is my brother."

Fleda was silent, thinking. Then she looked at Cerys uncertainly.

"If we drove you out, don't you hate us?" she asked.

Cerys gazed into the fire. "Hatred's like a burning log. If you hold onto it, it will destroy you. You can't be sure it will just affect those you hate. The flames spread where they will, beyond your control."

She didn't seem to want to say anything else, and so they sat together quietly, one on either side of the bed, watching over the king as he slept.

Markham Priory:
January 878

*T*HAT WAS IT. *All his monks and lay brothers were gone, to safety, he hoped. The caves had sheltered people in the past, and no doubt would do so again in the future. It had been difficult: they hadn't wanted to leave him. In the end, gently but firmly, he'd had to remind them of their vows of obedience, and reluctantly, with many backwards glances, they had gone. Even then, he'd suddenly remembered that he hadn't seen Cenred, the youngest of them. Matthew had gone straight to the hut where the garden tools were kept, knowing that that was where he would be. And sure enough, there he was, curled up in a corner, his bright brown eyes frightened but determined. Cenred had come to them after his family had been killed in a Danish raid, some years ago now, and had been like a faithful shadow treading in Matthew's footsteps, learning his skills with plants, listening to his words.*

"Let me stay!" he pleaded. "Or else you come too! I don't want to leave you!"

He'd hardly ever spoken so many words at once. Matthew put his hands on Cenred's shoulders and looked into his eyes.

"You will see me again," he said. "I will be here when you come back."

And in the end, Cenred had gone after the others.

Prior Matthew closed the door behind them. He wondered for a moment whether he should bar it, but decided there was probably no point. Even the thickest piece of wood wouldn't give pause to the visitors he was expecting.

He wondered how long it would be before they came. Young Francis, who had the keenest eyes of all of them, had yelled from the top of the church tower that he could see smoke rising from Barford, ten miles away. Matthew somehow felt certain that their leader would want to stay for a while and watch the destruction he had brought about. He had some time. Not much, but enough.

Matthew walked back towards the church through the priory garden. He had helped to lay it out, with its harmonious pattern of raised beds for herbs and vegetables, edged with narrow panels of woven willow and divided by neatly swept paths. In the very centre he had planted a rose bush, which in the summer bore sweetly scented white flowers. They were to remind the brothers of the purity of Our Lady, the Mother of Christ, as the thorns should make them think of the suffering of Christ on the cross. He hoped they did that, but even if they didn't – and he knew that most of the brothers were simple men, not much given to abstract thought – he felt that flowers deserved their place in the garden for their loveliness alone.

At this time of year, of course, the garden was sleeping. The feathery carrot tops just crept through their winter blanket of snow, and each tiny leaf on the thyme bush was edged with a delicate tracery of

138

frost. He looked more closely. Was that a glimmer of pale yellow under the purple sage bush? Perhaps his old eyes were deceiving him ... but no, it was the furled bud of a primrose. Even in the dark days of the year, new life was pushing its way through. Sighing deeply, he lifted his face to the sun, feeling its faint winter warmth like a blessing on his cheeks and forehead, and whispered his thanks to God for all the great splendours and tiny marvels He had created.

Then he walked into the church, kneeled in front of the altar, and began to pray.

Guthrum looked round the priory grounds suspiciously. Where were they all? If they'd run away, he hoped they hadn't taken all their treasures with him. If they had, that would make him cross, very cross indeed. Not that the pickings from a small establishment like this would amount to much.

"Find the grain and the food store," he growled to a group of his men. "These priests always look after their stomachs well enough. And the kitchen. See if they've been baking! Ivar, Thorkil, with me. Perhaps they're hiding in the church, expecting their milksop god to protect them."

He pushed open the heavy oak door. Funny how they built their churches better than their houses. This one was stone, sturdy and solid. He blinked. The interior was dark after the bright sunlight outside. Impatiently, he called over his shoulder for Ivar to open the door wider. He thought he could see something moving at the front.

The sun must have gone behind a tree or a cloud and then emerged, because suddenly a brilliant burst of light streamed though the doorway and lit up the altar and the figure standing in front of it.

139

Guthrum shaded his eyes uneasily. What was this?

It was a hooded figure, standing very still and tall, holding something in one hand. Its face was hidden.

Some long forgotten story stirred in Guthrum's memory. Something about three ancient women, the Norns, who lived at the ends of the earth and had the power of life and death over mortals. Their faces were always hidden, and you really didn't want to see what lay behind their hoods…

He took a step back, startling Ivar and Thorkil, who were close behind him. Annoyed, he got a grip of himself, drew out his short sword, and strode forward.

"You there — show yourself!"

The prior raised his head, and with his right hand pushed back his hood. With his left, he held firmly onto the large silver cross from the altar. Then he waited, his old face still and serene.

"Where are the others?" said Guthrum sharply.

"Gone," said the priest. "I made them go," he added.

"But you stayed," said Guthrum, suspiciously. "Why? You're going to die, you know."

The priest's milky blue eyes gazed at him calmly. "We're all going to die. It's just a question of when, and how."

"Fine," said Guthrum. "Let's make it now." He jerked his head back towards the others, and they moved forward.

The old man's arm, the one holding the cross, shot up into the air. The cross caught the light, so that it shone brilliantly.

"Wait!" he said.

Ivar and Thorkil hesitated.

"I have a request," continued the old man.

140

"Well?" snapped Guthrum.

"If I am to die, let it be by your hand, and yours alone. But first, I want you to look at me. Look me in the eyes. And then, if you can, you may kill me."

Guthrum respected bravery. And this man was brave, there was no denying that. Stupid perhaps, but brave. He stared into the pale blue of Father Matthew's eyes. And as he gazed, he seemed to see the great empty bowl of the sky, and the rippling surface of the ocean, and the level, shining shores of his homeland. It was so long since he had walked there, so long since he had seen his mother, his father, his wife. He had a sudden bleak sense of loss, of loneliness, as if a cold east wind whistled round his ears.

Abruptly, he turned away. Ivar and Thorkil almost fell over each other to give him room.

"There will be books," he snarled. "Find them. Burn them. Take any gold or silver. Do what you want to this place." He thrust his face close to theirs, his eyes glittering and fierce. "But as you wish to see your children's faces one day, leave him be!"

Then, ignoring their astonished faces, he marched out of the church without looking back.

Athelney: February 878

ALFRED HALF OPENED HIS EYES. His eyelids were heavy, and he still felt unutterably weary. But the feverish dreams, the flashes of pain and confusion, had eased. He looked round the room, trying to grasp where he was and what was happening. He saw Fleda by the fire, her golden head resting on her hand, sleeping.

A log collapsed into the fire. Fleda woke with a start and glanced over at him.

"Father – you're awake!"

He smiled and held out a hand to her. She took it in both hers, and gazed at him.

"Are you feeling better?" she asked anxiously. "You've been so ill…"

"I think I am," he said. He felt peaceful and quite happy, though somewhere, in the shadows at the back of his mind, he was vaguely aware that there were matters jostling for his attention.

She laid her head on his chest, and he stroked her hair,

admiring its brightness. Where had he seen that colour before? A smile lightened his face.

"I knew someone else once with hair like yours," he said softly, remembering. "Judith. She was a princess, like you. We were on our way back from Rome when I saw her for the first time. She was my friend, and then she became my stepmother. And then, I suppose, she was my sister-in-law."

Fleda's eyes widened and she sat up. "How could that be?"

"Well, it's a long story." Alfred leaned back against his sheepskins. "But we have time, don't we?"

It was two days since Alfred had woken and begun to feel better. He was still very weak, and Cerys wouldn't let Oswald or Erluin talk to him yet about the present or the future, but she was happy for him to explore the past with Fleda. So, bit by bit, he told her about Judith Martel and the Frankish court. She soon decided that she would have liked Judith very much, and was horrified when her father told her about Judith's betrothal to his father, Aethelwulf.

"But he was an old man," she said indignantly. "And she was your friend. How could he?"

"It was a matter of state – it was to seal the alliance between Francia and Wessex. Princesses aren't free to choose who they will marry – you know that."

Fleda frowned. "What – not at all?"

Alfred looked uncomfortable. "Well, not entirely. Though I would think that a marriage as – as uneven as that one, would be quite – well, unusual."

"I should certainly hope so," said Fleda. Then she said, "What relation would she be to me?"

Alfred considered. "She was my stepmother. So I suppose she would be your step-grandmother, if there is such a thing."

"And what happened to her? Was she unhappy with your father? Where is she now? Is she still alive?"

Her father held up his hands, laughing. "Too many questions!"

"I'm sorry. But I would have liked Judith. I know I would."

"I liked her too." He looked at Fleda, considering. "You remind me of her. She was good at being happy, even when it was hard, and you are, too."

Fleda felt pleased. "So," she prompted him. "What happened, after you found her in the garden?"

"Well, she and my father were married before we left Francia, and she was crowned queen at the same time – my father treated her with great honour. It was a very beautiful ceremony. When the archbishop put the crown on her head – it was a new one, specially made for her – he said this: 'May the Lord crown you with glory and honour, that the brightness of the gold and the gleam of the gems may always shine forth in your conduct and your acts…' I've always remembered those words," he

144

mused. "I didn't understand them at the time. I just liked the way they sounded. But now, I think perhaps they're meant to show what's important in a king or a queen: that it's what you do and what you are, and not what you have."

"Yes, but were they *happy*? And what about Baldwin?" urged Fleda impatiently.

"Ah," said Alfred. "Well, I'll come back to Baldwin. We haven't seen the last of him, don't worry. But first of all, before he came back into it, her story became tangled up with Aethelbald's. I told you about Aethelbald, didn't I? He was the oldest of us, and my father had left the kingdom in his care. But he didn't understand at all what it means to be a king. To him, it was just about power. He was a bully. He didn't understand that a king has duties, as well as rights..."

"Yes, yes," said Fleda, "but you were going to tell me what happened to Judith."

"What? Oh yes, Judith." His face softened again. "I *will* tell you. But I'm feeling a little tired at the moment. And quite hungry, too..."

Instantly contrite, Fleda ran off to fetch him some soup. Then while he rested, she helped Ulric to prepare the meal for later. He'd trapped rabbits and was going to cook them with onions and some roots that Cerys had brought from her garden. She'd promised that soon, when Alfred was better, she would take Fleda to see her house. She had never spent so long cooped up in such a small space, and though she enjoyed the time she spent talking to her father, she felt the need of a change.

It was obvious that the others were feeling the same. Ulric, Ricbert and Eadric ventured further and further away from the island, fishing and trapping, leaving Oswald and Erluin to guard the king. Oswald seemed contented enough. He was solid as a rock, Fleda thought. But he was gentle too. He watched Alfred patiently when he was at his weakest, taking turns with Cerys and Fleda, passing the time carving pieces of wood that he found on the island. Once, Fleda asked to see what he was making, and he showed her. It was a small boat, and the prow was in the shape of a swan, not the usual dragon. He had captured the lovely curve of its neck perfectly.

"It's for your brother," he explained. "He'll have lost his other toys when they left Chippenham, I expect."

Fleda was silent. There was a part of her that was afraid they might never see Edward again. But she touched the smooth wooden neck, and was glad that Oswald was preparing for a future that would contain them all.

She thought the waiting was hardest for Erluin. She knew he was desperate for news, and even more desperate to be doing something useful. He spent hours prowling round the island and practising sword strokes, but in the long dark evenings, when Ricbert, Eadric and Ulric kept themselves amused by setting each other riddles or telling stories, his face would grow dark and morose, and gradually his mood would infect the others and they would fall silent.

The weather didn't help. They hadn't seen the sun for days. The mist closed in on them, and dampness crept into their clothes, their bones, their minds.

But things were changing. The king was growing stronger. She sensed that all the time he was talking to her, his mind was working, gathering ideas, making plans. Soon, he would be ready to take command. They only had to be patient for a little longer.

It had to be true. Otherwise, what would become of them all?

After he had eaten some soup, Alfred stretched, flexing the muscles in his arms and fingers. They felt stiff, unused. Still, he could feel a tiny amount of strength seeping back into his limbs.

He sat up, and carefully swung his feet onto the floor. Holding onto the bed, he leant forward, trying to stand up. But the blood rushed to his head and pounded behind his eyes, and his legs felt weak and unsteady. Dizzily, he collapsed back down again – just as Fleda came back into the room. She flew at him, scolding him.

"Not yet! You're not strong enough to get up yet. You must wait till Cerys says."

He sat back, studying her face, not sure whether he should be amused or annoyed. With a slight shock of surprise, he realized that she had changed in the few weeks since they'd left Chippenham: she wasn't the child he remembered. "So," he said, "is the king to be ordered about by women?"

"For the time being, yes," she said firmly.

He shook his head, frowning. "This is no time to be idle."

"You don't have a choice," she pointed out. "You've been ill. Very ill. You have to rest first, and then you'll be better."

She studied him as he leaned back against the cushions. His eyes were clear and thoughtful, and his face, though still pale, had lost that frightening ashen colour. She felt suddenly relieved. He was himself again, as he had not been since they left Chippenham, and he was growing stronger. The time for stories by the fireside was almost done.

But not quite. "Judith," she prompted him, curling up on the end of the bed.

His face grew soft, as it always did when he spoke of Judith.

"It's as I said before – she knew how to be happy; it's a rare gift. And she knew how to make other people happy too. So, even though she really hadn't wanted to be married to my father, she didn't think about what she'd lost. Or at least, she didn't seem to. Who knows what she really felt? But she and my father..." He darted an uneasy glance at Fleda. "They were more like – not exactly

148

father and daughter, but not like husband and wife either.

"I think our court must have seemed quite backwards to her. After all, her great-grandfather, Charlemagne, was the Holy Roman Emperor. His kingdom stretched all the way across Europe, from Francia to Italy. His court was famed for the thinkers and philosophers it attracted. His Francia must have been a marvellous place.

"Judith was more of a scholar than any of us. I think she was quite shocked at how little we knew. When she left, she gave me a book, and she challenged me to learn how to read it. So I did. I found a priest to teach me. I'll always be grateful to her for that. Through books, we can learn the lessons of the past … and then we can work out how to safeguard the future…"

He lapsed into silence, clearly lost in his own thoughts. But Fleda wanted to know how Judith's story had ended. He sighed. "It's not a pretty story. My father died two years after the marriage, and then Aethelbald became king. And then…"

Alfred said nothing for a moment, but his face had turned dark and grim. "Even after all this time, it makes me angry," he said. "He'd no sooner become king than he seized Judith and forced her to marry him – an offence against God and the memory of our father, as well as against Judith. After two and a half years he was killed. Fighting a band of raiders, it was said. But no one actually saw him die. There were rumours, but no one tried too hard to find out the truth. He wasn't much mourned. Many felt that it was God's way of punishing him for what he'd done, to our father and to Judith."

His face was unreadable, and she shivered. It was another of those moments when Alfred wasn't her father any more, but a stranger with a cold face.

"Of course, I was only a child at the time," he added casually.

"And Judith?"

"His death set her free. She returned to Francia. And not long after that, I heard that she'd married Baldwin. Her father was against the marriage – I suppose he thought Baldwin wasn't good enough for her." He chuckled. "But Judith wasn't having any of that. She ran off with him."

"Oh!" said Fleda, pleased. "And was she happy?"

Alfred smiled. "I believe she was. He was a good man. A good fighter, too. They call him *Bras de Fer* – Iron Arm. King Charles, Judith's father, came to realize his value. But Judith died, some years ago – in childbirth, I believe."

He reached under the sheepskins he was leaning on and drew something out.

"This is the book she gave me," he said, stroking the leather cover tenderly. "I take it everywhere. I read the stories and they're full of familiar friends. It's meant a great deal to me. But now I'm going to give it to you."

She looked up, astonished, and he pushed her hair

back from her face and said seriously, "This has been a dark time for me. But you have made it lighter. I'm grateful for that, and I want you to have this book – Judith's book – so that you'll remember these days. And – this might sound a bit pompous, but it's a kind of pledge, too, for the future. Because when we've got rid of Guthrum – and we will – we're going to rebuild Wessex. I want the new Wessex to be a place where learning is valued, where it will thrive, just as it did years ago in Charlemagne's Francia."

"And what else do you want for Wessex?" said a cool, musical voice.

It was Cerys. She must have come in very quietly. She was leaning comfortably against the wall by the fire, her arms folded, her face in shadow.

Alfred was instantly alert and suspicious, and Fleda suddenly realized that he didn't recognize Cerys. In all the time she had spent caring for him, she had somehow never happened to be there when Alfred had been conscious. Fleda turned to her father and was about to speak, but before she could begin, Cerys moved forward into the light.

She looked extraordinarily tall and beautiful, with her strange, silver-grey eyes, and her hair which gleamed with the blue-black gloss of a raven's wing.

"You have no need to fear me," she said quietly. And then she seemed to draw shadow round her again and shrink to the size of an ordinary woman.

Alfred's face suddenly lit up.

"Cerys?" he said.

"No other!" she smiled. Then she sank into a curtsey. "Forgive me. I was forgetting that you are now a king."

"A king who's lost his kingdom, for the moment," he said wryly. There was a little silence, and then Alfred went on thoughtfully. "It's a long time since we met. You were mysterious then. And you still are."

"Perhaps. A little. But for the most part, just an ordinary woman."

"Has life treated you well?" he asked. He glanced at Fleda. "I know little of you, except, from what my daughter tells me, that you are a healer. And that I must thank you for your care of me."

"I have some skill. I'm glad it's been of use."

No one said anything for a moment. Alfred sat very still, waiting. Fleda looked from one to the other. They were both very powerful, she thought. Cerys had the power of forest pools and mist and growing things. But her father had the strength of an eagle, and its fierceness too. It was something she wasn't usually aware of, but it was there now, in the brooding intentness of his gaze.

"I had children," said Cerys abruptly.

Alfred said nothing, but he leaned forward slightly.

There was a look of pain in Cerys's eyes which Fleda had never seen before. Impulsively, Fleda went over to her. There was a bench near the fire, and Fleda touched Cerys's arm and guided her to it. She sat down beside her and took her hand. It was cold, in spite of the warmth of the fire. And Cerys was pale, her skin as translucent as ice.

"They were twins," she said. "Gwion and Caitlin. They were born in the spring, two years before you became king."

Fleda's eyes widened. That was the year she was born, too. What had happened to these children?

"Everyone thinks their own baby is beautiful," said Cerys softly. "Even when their ears stick out like cabbage leaves and their faces are as red and wrinkled as winter apples. But mine really were beautiful. Their heads were such a lovely shape. And their hands, their tiny, perfect fingers, tipped with little pink fingernails... Caitlin was noisy and nosy, always looking about her, kicking and waving her fists about as though she was in a hurry to get somewhere. But Gwion ... he was like one who had been in this world before, calm and wondering and wise. His eyes were like the underside of a cloud, grey, but a bright grey, as if there was a light behind that was trying to break through. I used to watch them as they slept – I loved the way their eyelashes rested on their cheeks. Their skin was so soft and delicate, like petals."

She took a deep breath, and her voice became clearer, yet more distant. "But they were born in the wrong year. The winter before, many had gone hungry. The summer had been dry early on, and then, when it was time to bring the harvest in, the rain came. Too much, too late.

Perhaps if the men had been here where they should have been, we could have saved some of the crops. But they were not here. They were off in Mercia, fighting with you and your brother."

Alfred stirred. "It was not a fight we chose. You know that. You know who we were fighting, and why. Would you rather we let the Danes run where they would, kill as they wished?"

"Of course not!" said Cerys passionately. "But when you throw a stone into a pool, it disturbs the water. It makes waves. And perhaps one of those waves carries away some small creature that was living its life on the shore, all unawares. You must remember that what you do has consequences. Perhaps, just perhaps, there are other ways to do things. I don't know what they might be – you're the king, that's your job."

Fleda held her breath. How dared Cerys speak to her father like this?

But he didn't explode, or even flare up. He stared at Cerys gravely. "Your children," he said. "What happened?"

Cerys sat silent and tense for a moment, as if she was gathering the strength to go on.

"The same thing happened the year that they were born. But it was even worse, because there were no stores left over from the year before. We'd eaten every grain of corn, every dried up apple, every scrawny chicken. When the weather turned cold, we had nothing to fight

154

it with. The old people went first, and then the children. My children."

She glanced at Fleda, and there was warmth in her gaze. "You have a daughter, my lord. I've seen her watching over you, caring for you. It's usually the other way round, isn't it? Parents care for their children.

"When you can't do that – when you have to watch them growing thinner and thinner, till you can see the bones beneath their skin – it's an unimaginably hard thing. It's a thing you never recover from."

Cerys straightened, and her strange silver eyes flashed a challenge at Alfred.

"Soon, you will be well. You will fight the Danes, and you will find a way to win. But that should be only the beginning. After that, what sort of country will you rule over? You speak of learning, and that's all very well, but what about the people? Can you make things better for them? If you can, and if they believe you can, they will follow you wherever you need to go. But if not…"

Alfred met her gaze. "I have been thinking of these things. I've made a beginning. But I know there is much more to be done, and that I will need help. I hope I will have yours." He paused, and then said gently, "I'm sorry for your loss."

"Yes," she said. "I see that you are."

She bowed her head, and then she was gone.

Alfred's eyes followed her.

"She speaks, and I listen," he said quietly. "Where does

155

her power come from? Who is she, really?"

Fleda smiled. "Oswald thinks she is a witch."

"But you don't?"

She was surprised by the serious note in his voice.

"Oh no. Not a witch."

"An enchantress, perhaps," he mused. "She certainly seemed like one all those years ago when we first met."

Fleda considered this. She remembered the flames, the first night Cerys had come to Athelney, how they'd dimmed suddenly and then danced. But perhaps that had happened just by chance. She decided not to mention it.

"She did tell me that she's British. And that Math, the reeve, is too. It seemed ... important to her. What does that mean, Father? I thought the British were our enemies. I thought they lived far away, in Cornwall and Wales. And yet..."

"And yet Cerys lives here, and is as much a part of this place as the reeds and the water birds. And is clearly not an enemy. Yes, it does seem puzzling, doesn't it?"

He leant back, and she jumped up guiltily.

"I'm sorry, Father – you're tired. You should sleep."

"No, no, I'm weak – nearly as weak as a kitten – but not sleepy. I've slept enough already. I'm just thinking. About what you said. About the British. It was their country once, you see. Ours now, of course ... but our ancestors came here from overseas. Many years ago – but still..."

Fleda sat silent for a little while, following this

thought. "So we fought them, and we won, and then it was our country?"

"Well – yes. You could put it like that, I suppose."

She followed the thought a little further. "And now the Danes have come from overseas, and it's us they're fighting, and if they win—"

"If they won – but they won't – it would be their country."

"And then will it happen again? Will someone else come?"

He frowned. "I hope not. But hope isn't enough, is it? It goes back to what Cerys was asking for. What she wants is a country at peace. But for a country to be peaceful, it has to be strong." He sighed. "There's a lot to think about, isn't there? Not just how to beat Guthrum, but what to do afterwards. And I still feel so feeble ... I think perhaps you were right after all. I should sleep."

After she'd gone, he wondered about Guthrum, where he was and what he was doing. Then, painfully, he thought of Ealswith and Edward and the little ones again. Were they still in Winchester? Were they safe?

Alfred swung his feet onto the floor and took a deep breath. Putting a hand out to the wall, he slowly, carefully, leant forward and began to straighten himself. His legs felt ridiculously weak, and he bit his lip in frustration. He managed to stand for only a moment before he fell back onto the bed.

It was a tiny bit better than the first time he'd tried.

He was getting stronger.

But it was too slow, far too slow. There was so much to do – so much he needed to know!

How much time did he have? What was happening, out there beyond the marshes?

It was a very long time before he slept that night.

Out of the Dark:
February 878

THE NEXT DAY, when Ulric came in to make up the fire, Alfred stopped him.

"No," he said. "Never mind that. I want you to find me my clothes, and then help me to get over to the main hut."

Ulric's face lit up. "My lord! You're feeling better!"

"Yes indeed. A little shaky, but that will pass. As time is passing. So – if you can find me my tunic and trousers and boots, and if your shoulder's strong enough for me to lean on, we'll be off."

Ulric beamed. He opened his mouth to say something, but then realized he had no idea what he should say. He had been in and out constantly throughout Alfred's illness, tending to the fire, bringing food and drink, taking it away again – doing whatever Cerys and Fleda asked him to do. But this was the first time the king had been alert enough to speak to him.

Alfred raised a questioning eyebrow, and Ulric

spluttered, "Yes, my lord! Right away, my lord!"

And soon they were outside in the winter sunlight. Alfred was leaning heavily on Ulric, and after a few steps, he paused and looked round, breathing deeply. It was less cold than it had been when they first arrived, but the dreary weather of the last few days had given way to a pale sun, and some of the distant meadows were pale with frost. Alfred gazed across the marches, enjoying the touch of the cool air on his face. Then his eyes narrowed, and he straightened up, wincing as he used muscles that had been idle for too long.

"Someone's approaching the island," he said tensely. "See that boat, over there, on the far side of the water?" Ulric had already drawn his knife from his belt, but Alfred touched his arm, calming him.

"It's probably all right. Just Math, or someone from the village. All the same – where are the others?"

When they entered the main hut, Oswald, Erluin and the rest of the king's thegns were sitting round the table eating breakfast and talking. Oswald was facing the door, and when he saw Ulric and Alfred in the doorway, his mouth dropped and his eyes widened. The others turned quickly to see the cause. For a moment, there was an astonished silence, and then everyone jumped up and spoke at once. But it was Oswald who reached the king first.

Alfred grinned. "Well, old friend. Nothing to say?"

Oswald dashed his hand roughly across his eyes,

and cleared his throat.

"I'm not a poet. I don't have a word hoard. But…" A huge grin spread over his face. "By all the saints, I'm glad to see you on your feet again!"

Alfred smiled. "No more than I am, believe me! But listen – someone is coming here."

They were instantly grim-faced and alert, and while Oswald settled Alfred comfortably in the high-backed settle beside the fire, the others went outside. Soon Ricbert, who was noted for his keen eyesight, came back inside and reported that the visitors were Math and another man he didn't recognize.

"Why is he bringing a boat?" frowned Oswald. "The place is choked with reeds and whatnot. The man's a fool – he'll never get a boat through that lot."

Erluin winced. "Whatever else he is, Math is certainly not a fool. And he knows this place. There must be a way through."

Fleda had taken to sleeping in a hut that had previously been used as a store room, which Cerys also used when she stayed overnight. It was close to her father's, and she slipped in to see him when she woke.

Finding him gone, she was puzzled for only a moment before she realized that he must have felt well enough to go to the communal hut. She felt a tiny pang of regret. Of course, she was delighted at his recovery – but she had enjoyed being the one he talked to. Already,

161

she was beginning to miss him.

She wandered out into the sunshine. In a few weeks it would be spring, and the beginning of the fighting season. Though under Guthrum's new rules, it seemed that the killing season was whenever he wanted it to be.

Something caught her eye, down below, and she saw Math's boat. She watched as he steered it skilfully through the reeds, then she ran down the bank to meet him. Towards the bottom of the hill she almost stumbled into a grassy ditch which she hadn't noticed before. She thought of Edward suddenly, and smiled. They could have had good games here, hiding in the ditch – it was plenty deep enough – and pretending they were on opposite sides, with one of them defending the hill against the other. Her smile faded. It seemed a long time since she'd played. But just as she began to wonder where Edward was and what he was doing, she saw that Math was pulling his boat out of the water.

He smiled at her and sketched a bow. "Forgive me if I don't kneel, my lady, but the ground is rather wet!"

"Kneel?" she asked in surprise. "Why would you want to kneel to me?"

"Because you are your father's daughter," he answered seriously, "and because the other day, you brought a roomful of grown men to their senses, and made us think about what is important. And I'm here again because of that." He turned to indicate the man who had come with him. "This is Wulf. He's the best carpenter in Wessex, bar none. You need defences, and he's the man to build them."

Wulf smiled. He had iron-grey hair, bushy eyebrows and a creased forehead, and was shorter and sturdier than Math. He hooked his thumbs into his belt and looked round. His eyes narrowed, and he nodded sagely towards the ground at Fleda's feet. "You've found the ditch," he said wisely. "We can use that."

"Use it?" she said, puzzled.

He nodded again. "Been used before," he volunteered. "Many times, I shouldn't wonder. It's an old place, this is. Athelney. The Island of Princes."

Fleda remembered that her father had said something similar when they first arrived. "Oh yes!" she said. "My father's island!"

But he was shaking his head. "No. Princes from long ago. Nearly forgotten now. But not quite. Not by every-one."

"Oh," said Fleda, rather inadequately.

"It's an island of many peoples," explained Math. "Many tribes. A rich mix."

"Athelney?" asked Fleda, confused.

"No," he chuckled. "Not Athelney. Britain."

She thought about what Alfred had been saying the night before, about the Saxons and now the Danes. And there were the British, like Cerys and Math himself. And now, it seemed, there were these others who had been there before – or were they the British too? It was very muddling.

"Yes," Wulf was saying sagely. "A ditch and a palisade, that's what we need. Enough to keep anybody out. If they get this far," he added.

"Yes," nodded Math. "Best if they don't."

Fleda took a deep breath. "My father is much better," she said brightly. "Shall I take you to him?"

Oswald was standing ostentatiously on guard outside the communal hut. He nodded to Math, and asked who Wulf was. He looked Wulf up and down and pointed to the axe stuck in his belt.

"That stays out here," he said gruffly.

"Tools," pointed out the little man. "I'm a carpenter."

"Yes, but—"

"This is the king's man," explained Math to Wulf. "It's his job to protect him." There was nothing wrong with the words, but Fleda caught the note of mockery in Math's voice and knew he was reminding Oswald of his last visit, when he'd arrived unobserved – and she saw by his scowl that Oswald had noticed it too.

Wulf hesitated, but finally took the axe out of his belt and leant it tenderly against the wall of the hut. Then Fleda led them in to see her father.

Alfred was pale and still had circles under his eyes and hollows in his cheeks, but he sat straight-backed, with his shoulders squared and a lively gleam in his eyes that made her smile with relief.

Math kneeled before him. He had his sister's grace,

and the gesture was elegantly done. But when he looked up at Alfred, the expression on his face was guarded. He might have bent his knee, thought Fleda with sudden clarity, but he was not yet wholly sure of her father.

Alfred smiled at Math.

"So. I have been ill, as you know. I hear that you are going to help us." Math made as if to speak, but Alfred held up a hand to stop him. "I know that you have doubts, and we will speak of these. But you must know this, Math." The room was silent, holding its breath. "The choice is very simple. On the one hand, there are the Danes. I've been twice lost – lost in these marshes, and lost in my illness. So I don't know exactly what they're doing, or how much destruction they've caused. But I can guess. And on the other hand, there's myself, just as you see me." His hand swept round, in a gesture that included the simple room and the small band of thegns. "But I promise you this. All that I am is at the service of the people of this country – the English peo-ple. And by the English, I mean all those who count these islands their home." He paused. "And I am all that you have. It's either me, or the Danes. There's no one else. So, Math. Are you with me, or against me?"

Math's face was without its usual glint of mockery, and he spoke quietly. "I have already said that I will fight for you, my lord. The doubts you speak of are not about that."

"Then...?"

165

Math was silent for a moment. His forehead was furrowed, and Fleda could see that he was trying to find the right words.

"If a house is burned down, my lord, it is a tragedy – or at least a great inconvenience. When its owners come to build it again, they can if they wish make it exactly the same as it was before. But if they are wise, they will make it better. Perhaps they'll make it bigger, or of different materials, or perhaps they'll build the fireplace in such a way that the fire doesn't smoke so much. What of your house, my lord?"

"My house will be different," said Alfred simply. "It will be better. But unless I can drive the Danes back once and for all, it will be nothing but a heap of ashes on the ground, soon to blow to nothingness in the wind." He leant forward and stared intently at Math. "I asked you a question, and I need your answer. We have no room for a doubter. Are you with us, or not?"

For once, there was no hint of laughter, mocking or otherwise, in Math's face. "I am with you, my lord," he said gravely. And they clasped hands.

Alfred looked round at them all. *This is it*, he thought. *This is where it begins. The wind has changed, Guthrum. It's been filling your sails for far too long. My turn now!*

"This is the beginning," he said. "The beginning of the way back. There aren't many of us here. But we have a common cause, and every one of you has a true heart and enough courage to beat a hundred thousand Danes." He

166

grinned. "Fortunately that won't be necessary. Because out there are hundreds – no, thousands – more such as you. All they need is a leader, to bring them and bind them together. Math – I believe you were to send messages to Aethelnoth?"

Math nodded. "He was overjoyed to hear that you still live, my lord. He is yours to command." He hesitated, and Alfred looked at him sharply.

"Say what's in your mind," he urged.

"I think that many people believe you are dead or – or gone, my lord. As Burgred of Mercia is gone, overseas to safety."

"You mean they think I've run away?" he said, beginning to look angry.

"It's been some weeks since you left Chippenham, sir. Nothing has been heard of you, and Guthrum roams where he chooses."

They were all sitting round the table now. It was a council of war, thought Fleda – the first she had ever attended. She sat very quietly, in case anyone noticed she was there and thought she shouldn't be. Alfred rested his elbows on the table and clasped his hands under his chin thoughtfully.

"You have a suggestion, I think."

"The people need to see you, my lord. Aethelnoth is the ealdorman. He could order the reeves of every hundred in Somerset to raise their men and instruct them to take up arms. But unless they are convinced that ... well, that you can win – he will have only limited success."

Oswald's face was a picture of outrage, but Erluin was listening with interest and Alfred was nodding thoughtfully. "Yes. I understand. But I can't go round to every hundred court in Somerset – and then there are the other shires too, there's Wiltshire, Hampshire, Devon, Dorset."

"Perhaps they need a demonstration," said Erluin, frowning in concentration. "Something to show beyond doubt that you're still a force to be reckoned with."

"Yes!" said Fleda, her face alight. "They don't all have to see us, they just have to hear of us! All we have to do is think of something that will make a good story, and then everyone will hear of it and want to be part of it!"

A circle of surprised faces looked at her, and she put her hand over her mouth, remembering she'd meant not to be noticed. But Erluin grinned at her.

"Exactly so! Something daring – something unexpected."

"We need to do both," decided Alfred. "We need to reach as many people as we can, and we need to show them that we can do what's needed. But before we can do either, we need to know where Guthrum is, how many men he's got, what he's planning – what he's thinking. We need spies. Math, your people will help? Good." He turned to Wulf. "The island is well hidden and I doubt the Danes will find us. But just in case, we must have fortifications. What do you think, Wulf the woodman? Can you help us?"

"You've got a ditch," said Wulf stolidly. "Need a fence now, a strong, high one. And a platform this side, so you can defend it. Easy enough. Plenty of wood. Trees all over the place."

"Oh. Right," said Alfred, looking taken aback by Wulf's directness. "Er – good. So you'll do that for us?"

Wulf nodded. "Yes. Not alone though. Need more men." He glanced round the table. "This lot'll do, for a start. Can bring more tomorrow."

There was some grumbling, but Wulf cheerfully ignored it and led off the cream of the king's bodyguard to chop and split wood. After they'd gone, Alfred leaned back and closed his eyes, and Fleda went to him, concerned.

"Father – are you all right?"

He opened his eyes, looking tired but cheerful, and smiled at her.

"Don't worry. I'm getting stronger every minute. I feel hungry, though – is there any food about?"

"Yes," said Fleda, "Ulric made some pottage. I don't know what we'd do without him; he can make food out of almost nothing. Which is just as well," she observed ruefully, "because I think nothing is pretty much what we have. We'll have to ask the villagers for more food soon..."

"And I expect they will have little enough to give," said Alfred, thoughtfully. He ate his broth and then asked her to find him a stick so that he could lean on it while his legs got used to walking again.

"No time for weakness now," he said briskly. "Sometimes, Fleda, life's like climbing a mountain in the mist with a great pack on your back. And other times, it's like being on a ship – Cerdic's ship! – with the wind behind you and the tide taking you where you want to go. The tide's turned for us – I'm sure of it!"

The next day, men came from Aller and other nearby villages. They had come to help build the palisade, and soon the island was alive with the sounds of sawing and hammering and men's voices.

Someone else came too. Someone they hadn't been expecting.

His name was Björn, and he was the blacksmith from Chippenham – the same man who had been dragged before Guthrum as the Viking chief stood gazing at Alfred's deserted manor house on Twelfth Night.

Math brought him in the boat. He was blindfolded and his hands were tied, and one of Math's men sat behind him with a knife ready, just in case he turned out not to be who he said he was. But Erluin looked at him with interest, and vouched for him.

"Yes, I know this man," he said. "He's a good smith – none better." He drew his sword, and balanced it on the palms of his hand. "He made this. See? Beautifully balanced. A lovely piece of work."

Oswald looked suspiciously at Björn. "That's as may

be," he growled, "but what's he doing here? How did he know where to come?" He glared at Math. "You shouldn't have brought him. What were you thinking of?"

Math sighed. "How else were we to know if he is who he says he is? And if he has turned spy, he won't live to carry tales to his master." The threat hung in the air for a moment, and then Cerys appeared, emerging from the mist that clung to the island almost constantly now that the weather had turned milder. She stopped short when she saw the smith, taking in the blindfold, the bound hands and the threatening knife, and looked a question at Math.

"He says he's a smith from Chippenham, come to serve the king."

"And you don't believe him?" She walked towards the stranger, but Oswald stepped forward to block her path.

"You'd do well to be cautious! What do we know of him, except what he tells us?"

Their eyes locked, but Oswald's fell first. He shrugged and let her pass.

She stepped up to the smith, and untied the blindfold. He blinked, startled by the sudden sunlight. He was not a tall man, but his chest and shoulders were broad and powerful. She looked searchingly at him, and he stared back at her steadily, his eyes bleak and sad, his shoulders drooped and weary. After a few moments she gestured to Math.

"You can untie his hands. He has nowhere to go but here."

Fleda watched, fascinated. How could Cerys know that just from looking at him? She stared at him, to see if she too could read his face.

It was empty. There seemed to be no feeling there at all, just a deadness in his eyes, and she shivered. If she'd been in his position, she would have been angry, resentful, perhaps frightened. But he seemed to be none of those things. She thought he reminded her of someone, and for a moment couldn't think who it was. But then out of the corner of her eye she noticed Ulric, who was watching the smith with a troubled expression in his eyes, and she remembered how Ulric had looked when he spoke of his family, and of wanting to watch Guthrum die. And she realized it wasn't emptiness she could see: it was despair, the death of feeling. This man really didn't care what happened to him.

Impulsively, she went over to him and touched his arm, hardly noticing that Oswald and the others had moved forward protectively.

"Please," she said. "Come inside. Tell us what has happened to you."

Cerys nodded slightly, and they led him in to meet the king.

When he saw Alfred, he hesitated, and then sank rather awkwardly to his knees. He kept his head bowed for a while, and when he finally began to speak, there was a slight tremor in his voice. Then Fleda realized that, just as with Ulric, it wasn't so much that he felt too little;

it was more that he felt too much.

"My lord," he whispered, "I was afraid that you were dead, and that we were all lost."

And then Björn told them his story.

"It was snowing, the day the Northmen came. I was up early. I had a lot of work on – it's always good for business when you are in residence, my lord. I wanted to get the fire going; it has to be good and hot, as you'll know. And so there I was, up and about when most people were still snoring in their beds.

"I hadn't been up long when I heard the pounding of horses' hooves. They were muffled, because of the snow, but there was no mistaking the sound. It seemed strange, so early and in the Christmas season. I went to the door, but by the time I stuck my head outside there was practically nothing to see – just a cloud of snow, drifting in the dark. I wondered what all the hurry was, but then I thought, well, no matter – what do I know about the ways of the great? And I went back to tending my fire with the bellows.

"A couple of hours later, I heard the same sound. Except it wasn't quite the same. It was louder, much louder, ten, twenty, fifty times louder. And it was all mixed up with yelling and shouting. I didn't look outside that time. I didn't need to – I knew. It all made sense then; it was our turn, and you had gone, and you'd left us to face them." He had been looking down at his hands as he spoke, but now he looked up.

Alfred met his eyes, and didn't flinch.

"My wife was carrying our first child. She was my first thought, my first fear. I had an outhouse out the back, where I kept the wood and the charcoal. Gytha was terrified, because she realized what was happening, but she did as I told her – I made her crouch down in a tiny space behind the woodpile and promise to stay there and not make a sound or move a muscle till I came back for her. Then I went back into the shop, picked up an iron bar, and waited.

"I don't know why they came for me in particular. Maybe they saw the smoke coming from the roof. I think they'd just been told to find someone – anyone – who could tell them what had happened, where you'd gone. They smashed down the door with their axes, and my iron bar could have been a toy sword for all the use it was. I could see the bloodlust in their eyes, but they didn't kill me – well, you can see that! They dragged me to the green, and Guthrum was there, in front of your hall, gazing at it. He asked me if I knew where you'd gone, if I'd seen or heard anything, and I looked him in the face and lied – I told him you'd ridden east.

"He said I'd be useful because I'm a smith, and so they let me go. But before I got back to the house I could see the glow of the flames. The forge was burning. All that mattered to me was Gytha and the baby, and I ran round to the outhouse to find her."

He paused, looking down at his hands, which were

174

large and strong. He curled them into fists, so tight that the skin stretched white over his knuckles.

"It was too much for her, the shock. She lost the baby. And then she took a fever, and inside three days she was dead too."

"What did you do?" asked Cerys gently.

"I buried her in the night, in the churchyard. The ground was frozen hard, but there were those who were brave enough to help me. The Danes were busy feasting and drinking anyway – they didn't care about us.

"And then I left."

He paused, and then went on. "Guthrum said you'd run away, my lord. He said he was the king now. I thought, well, either it's true, and there's no hope, or it's not true, and sooner or later, you'll fight back. And if you're going to fight back, you'll need weapons making; you'll need a smith. So I decided to come looking for you. I knew you'd gone west, but I didn't know where. I asked people along the road, and there were some who said they'd seen a band of horsemen on Twelfth Night – others whispered of ghosts, riding on the storm, cloaked with snow. Just whispers, rumours, nothing certain.

"The trail led to the summer country. Then, in Aller, I overheard two women talking about strange lights they'd seen out in the marshes in the evening. They were afraid – they spoke of ghosts! And I began to wonder, and to ask one or two questions." He nodded towards Math. "Next thing I knew, I was given a very unfriendly greeting by your man there. And now, at last, here I am."

"Here and welcome," said Alfred gravely. "You were quite right – there is a great fight ahead of us, and we *will* need weapons. Your skill will be invaluable to us. You must tell us what you need to make them, and we shall see how we can obtain it."

Björn looked at him, and for the first time there seemed to be a spark glimmering at the back of his eyes.

"So Guthrum was wrong, my lord?"

Alfred nodded. "As wrong as he could be. The last battle's already begun. He just doesn't know it yet."

It was all very exciting – or at least, thought Fleda a little resentfully, it was for some people. There was an atmosphere of brisk and purposeful activity about the island now. The smith had explored all the outbuildings, looking for a suitable place to start building a new forge, and had been delighted to discover one was already there. It was in a dark and dusty hut piled high with cobweb-encrusted rubbish that had been accumulating for years.

"It just needs a bit of fixing up," he declared. "And then all I need is a steady supply of charcoal and plenty of iron – and there's quite a bit of stuff here I can melt down to start off with. Oh, and I'll need an assistant. I can make you swords and knives with the sharpest edge you could wish to feel, but for that I'll need steel, and someone to help me weld the steel to the iron. You have to be quick for that job, and you need two pairs of hands."

Ulric said shyly that he knew a little about using a forge. There had been a small one on the farm which they'd used for making and mending tools and pots and pans.

Soon he and Björn were busy clearing out the hut. They got on well; they shared a hatred of Guthrum. But Fleda felt a little bereft; she and Ulric hadn't spent a lot of time together, but he had been kind to her, and he was the only one who was anywhere near her age.

Alfred's thegns were busy too. They were supervising the building of the defences, and organizing the local men into making shafts for arrows and axes and short spears. Others trapped water birds, to steal their feathers for arrow flights.

Of course, Fleda wasn't expected to do any of these things. In fact, it was a bit difficult to know what she was expected to do. She had thought at first that she would be able to take Ulric's place as cook, but her skills were very limited, and with the increasing number of mouths to feed, it quickly became obvious that the task was beyond her. So Wulf brought his wife over to take charge of the kitchen.

Alfred was getting stronger all the time. At first, he had to lean on his stick as he walked around, but soon he was able to manage without it. He moved among the men, laughing with them and encouraging them, and the atmosphere was very different to how it had been just a few weeks ago. They had moved from despair to hope, from darkness to light.

As wonderful as it was, sometimes Fleda missed the times she and her father had shared. They had grown close during the dark days of his illness, and she had become used to being someone with an important part to play, someone whose views were worth listening to. Now everyone was treating her like a child again, like someone of no importance. It wasn't enough. She knew now what it was to be at the centre, and a place on the edge wouldn't do.

There came a day when the sound of hammering stopped. At last the fence was finished. It was a sturdy barricade, with a platform behind it. It would be easy to see if anyone was approaching. If a fight became necessary, they would have the advantage. The attacker would have to negotiate first the deep ditch, then the tall barricade. If they made it past that, the defenders would be waiting above them, with all sorts of unpleasant surprises ready to rain down on them.

But the best defence was still the country itself. No one who was unsure of their way would think to venture into the inhospitable and treacherous marshes. Alfred and his followers were as safe as they could be anywhere.

Soon after the fence was finished, Math came to meet Alfred. Fleda was curled up with Judith's book, and she was tracing the words with a finger and sounding them out silently. She looked up as a shadow fell across the page. It was her father.

"Math tells me that Aethelnoth has news for us. I've suggested we should meet at Glastonbury, at the abbey. I wanted to go there anyway, to ask the abbot for his blessing. Would you like to come too? Cerys will be with us." He paused. "We'll leave in the morning, early. Keep to your boy's clothes – we travel in secret, and a boy on the road will attract less attention than a girl."

He smiled and was gone. He never had much time to stop and talk these days.

Still, a journey! *That* was good! She went outside and searched the horizon. There was Glastonbury, where the sky met the earth. A ribbon of mist covered the lower slopes of the hill, so that it looked as if it was floating: magical and serene. She'd had enough of being cooped up on Athelney: it would be good to leave the island.

Glastonbury:
March 878

THEY WERE TO GO TO GLASTONBURY by boat, and Oswald was extremely unhappy about it.

"I don't mind proper boats," he complained, "but that's nothing but an overgrown bucket!"

Math grinned. "It's a punt, and it's perfectly safe. Even for someone your size! In you get – steady now!" The boat rocked, and Fleda laughed as Oswald's arms flailed wildly.

Alfred went with Math and Oswald, while Cerys and Fleda had a smaller punt to themselves. Fleda watched, fascinated, as Cerys propelled it skilfully through the reeds, wielding the paddle with both hands in a smooth circular movement. Soon, they were out into a stretch of open water. Flocks of birds had been riding the ripples placidly, but as the punts moved among them, they lifted off, reeling up into the sky with indignant squawks, and as Fleda turned to watch them, she realized that she could no longer tell where Athelney was: it was lost in the marshes.

When they'd first come to Athelney, it had been dark and everything had seemed strange. Since then she'd become used to the island, but now, out in the open, she realized afresh how remote and strange this country was. It was neither completely water, nor wholly land: it was a place between two worlds. The wide levels of water, a gleaming mirror reflecting the sky, were edged with reeds and clumps of willow and alder, their thin winter branches etched against the sky. In some places, the trees grew in a line, and she wondered whether in the summer, when the waters went down, as everyone said they would, these would form the border of a meadow. Or perhaps they marked a trackway, like the one between Athelney and Lyng. How could you ever really know a place that changed so much from season to season? Perhaps that was why there was this touch of mystery about Math, and particularly Cerys: maybe they just reflected the shifting nature of the land they lived in, as the ripples reflected the dappled gilt sunlight.

She realized that they were stopping: they'd reached a low ridge of hills, and they had to get out of the punts and pull them up out of the water. Fleda watched, impressed, as Math and Cerys hoisted the boats onto their shoulders.

"You must be very strong," she said to Cerys.

"Oh, I am!" grinned Cerys. "But you don't need much strength to carry a punt. They're as light as a feather."

181

And she explained that they were constructed of hide stretched over a framework made of thin pieces of willow – not of solid wood, like ordinary boats.

"Why do we have to carry them?" asked Oswald. "Can't we just hide them in the undergrowth, and pick them up when we come back?"

"Glastonbury's almost an island," said Cerys. "Ynys Witrin is its old name – the Isle of Glass. You can reach it by road, but from this direction, the easiest way to get there is by boat. We just have to cross these hills – it's not far – and then we can take to the boats again."

"Then I will carry your boat," said Oswald firmly, "light or not."

Cerys glanced at him, considering. "That's a kind thought, and I thank you for it!" And as he shouldered the boat she dropped him a curtsey, which was only slightly mocking.

It was good to be out in the open, with solid earth beneath her feet and the sun on her cheeks, and Fleda was quite sorry when they reached the water and took to the boats again. But then Cerys asked her if she would like to try her hand with the paddle, and the time passed quickly as she tried to master this new skill.

When they reached Glastonbury, she realized with a slight sense of disappointment that the hill, or tor, as Math called it, was much smaller than she had expected. From Athelney, it had seemed to tower over the surrounding levels and, as Oswald had said, it had a way of drawing your eye to it. But close up, it was really quite small. She said as much to Cerys.

"Yes," she agreed. "That's true. All the same, if you climb it, you can see more than you would imagine." She paused. A little smile played at the corners of her mouth, and she flashed a silver-eyed glance at Fleda. "And I don't just mean that you can see a long way – although you can, a remarkably long way."

Fleda was puzzled. "What *do* you mean, then?"

"I mean that you can sometimes see things on the tor that you are unlikely to see anywhere else – or so people say."

Math, who was walking just ahead of them, glanced round, frowning. "Is this wise, Cerys?" he asked.

She chuckled. "Don't worry, brother. It's only a story – an old, old story, which people tell to pass the time!" But all the same, Fleda noticed that she dropped a little further back, so that they were out of earshot of Alfred and Oswald.

"The story goes," she began, "that the tor is hollow. And that it is an entrance to the Otherworld, the world of the fairies, which is ruled over by Gwyn ap Nudd. At certain times of the year, if you were to go up there at dusk, you might see them dancing. They love to dance, in circles, weaving round and round. If they like the look of you, they may let you in. And then you'll find yourself in a palace, finer by far than any of your father's. The walls sparkle with crystal and precious gems, and Gwyn

183

sits on a throne made of solid gold. There is music to delight your ear, delicious food to tempt your appetite, and fountains of the clearest water to quench your thirst.

"The fairies can give you whatever you wish for: beauty, good luck – or maybe just a cow to provide you with an endless supply of the creamiest milk. But there is always a price. You have to promise something in return, and if you break your word, they are merciless – they'll take away whatever they gave you, and more besides."

Fleda's eyes were wide. "Is it true? Have you seen them?"

"No, she has not," said Math firmly. "And you had better not mention them when you get to the abbey. Fairies belong to an earlier age, and the monks do not appreciate the idea that they are close neighbours to such unchristian creatures. They even built a chapel up there and dedicated it to St Michael, who is God's warrior angel, so that he could keep guard against them."

"Yes," said Cerys mischievously, "but somehow it's never been very successful, has it? No one uses it. Perhaps the air's too strong for the monks up there!"

The shore of the lake was busy with a market, and no one noticed them among the crowds of people sifting through the piles of goods for sale on the stalls. Fleda longed to join them. Glastonbury was a busy port: though it was inland, ships sailed upriver with all kinds of goods, and merchants came to the market buying and selling. She could see piles of scarlet, purple and turquoise silks, barrels of wine, and piles of furs. One pelt she saw was pure white, and with a little surge of excitement she remembered her father speaking of great white bears that roamed the northern snows. She'd thought it was just a traveller's tale, but here was proof that it was true.

"Can't we stop and look?" she asked Cerys eagerly.

But Cerys shook her head and said she was sorry, but she had errands to do, people to see.

"Anyway," she added, "I don't think the monks would want a woman treading on their sacred ground – I don't think they're much keener on women than they are on Gwyn ap Nudd!"

Fleda was disappointed. It seemed a waste to come to Glastonbury and then have to spend her time in the abbey. She'd had enough of peace and quiet in Athelney. But Cerys clearly didn't want company, so, reluctantly, she turned and followed her father.

The gate to the abbey was closed, and they had to ring a bell to ask for admittance. A shutter at shoulder height opened, and a monk peered out. His thin, dark face had a pinched, nervous look, but when Math spoke to him, his face relaxed into recognition and he opened the gates and let them in. There was something about him that made Fleda feel uneasy: his eyes slid away from a direct gaze.

He rang a bell, and a second monk with a comfortable-looking stomach and several chins came bustling up to greet them.

"Welcome!" he said. "I am Uhtred, the cellarer, and it is my happy duty – and may I say, my very great pleasure – to see to your comfort during your visit to us." He glanced round, and lowered his voice. "The abbot had word from Aethelnoth, the ealdorman, that you were to grace us with your presence; really, it is most unexpected, and such a – such a very great..." He was clearly so excited at being in the presence of the king that he was almost – but not quite – lost for words. Alfred smiled, and put his finger to his lips.

"Truly, the honour is mine," he said. He looked round, his face eager and curious, and said to Fleda, "You remember I told you about going to Rome with my father?"

She nodded.

"Well, Rome is the capital city of Christendom," he said, "and it has the grave of St Peter. But Glastonbury has perhaps an even greater claim to fame – did you know that?" Not waiting for an answer, he went on, looking round at the smooth emerald-green lawns that surrounded the abbey. "It's said that Joseph of Arimathea came here. Joseph was the great-uncle of Christ himself, and he helped to take Our Lord's body down from the cross. He was a wealthy merchant, and he'd had a fine stone tomb prepared for when his own time came. But he gave it up so that Christ's body would be properly sheltered. And afterwards, he travelled far and wide on his ships, and eventually his ship came to Glastonbury."

"Why?" said Fleda. "Why did he come here, in particular?"

Alfred turned to the monk. "It's a good question, and I must admit, I don't know the answer to it. What about you, Father Uhtred? Do you?"

Father Uhtred beamed at Fleda. "Indeed, it *is* a good question!" he said approvingly. "Probably he came here looking for lead. The Mendips – that range of hills which you can see in the distance – are a good source of lead, which the ancients needed for their great buildings. And – may I show you something? I know that you have important matters that you must be eager to discuss, but it would only take a moment..."

Alfred hesitated, but it would have been hard to deny Father Uhtred's enthusiasm. He nodded, and the monk led them quickly to a small, gnarled tree, whose branches were scattered with a few small silver-white blossoms.

The monk stood beside it and looked at them expectantly. "Do you notice anything?"

"It's a hawthorn, isn't it?" ventured Oswald. "It's flowering a bit ahead of time, though. It's not spring yet."

Father Uhtred looked delighted. "Oh, but it isn't early – it's late! This is not an English hawthorn – it comes from the banks of the River Jordan in Palestine. And it flowers not only at Easter, but at Christmas-time. Joseph had a trusty staff made of thorn wood, such as any of us might like to lean on when we grow old and weary. He leant on it so hard when he first landed here that it sank into the ground and took root – and there it stands still, after all these centuries!"

They all stood and gazed at the tree respectfully.

"And there's more," he continued. "There is another story that when Jesus was growing up, his great-uncle took him on some of his voyages. So it may be – certainly I believe it's possible – that this land has been trodden on by the very feet of Christ!"

Math and Alfred had heard the story before, but it was new to Oswald as well as to Fleda, and the two of them gazed in awe-struck silence at the grass, as if they expected it to be flattened at any moment by mystical footprints.

But then there was a clang as the gates opened again, and the sound of men's voices, and the moment of peace was broken. It was the ealdorman, Aethelnoth, come to talk of war.

Aethelnoth was tall and spare, with sharp cheekbones and a thin, intelligent face. His hair was mostly grey, but Fleda thought he was probably not much older than her father. Alfred strode up to him and stretched his arms wide as if to hug him, but Aethelnoth was already sinking to one knee, his face alight as he gazed at Alfred, who laughed.

"Come now – it's not so long since we saw each other

– last year, in Wareham, was it not? And you played your part there as you always have, ever since you came hunting with me not far from here, when my brothers would not!"

Aethelnoth stood, and they clasped hands. "That's true, my lord. But a good deal has happened since then. After Chippenham, when we heard nothing of you for all these weeks, we thought – well, we were afraid you were dead. And then when Math told us that you were not only alive, but here in the heart of the summer country, it was all he could do to stop us riding to you straight away." He glanced at Math. "But he was right. For the time being, you must stay hidden. Secrecy is your best defence, and your strongest weapon. Guthrum knows you are the one he has to destroy; you are the one searches for, all the time and everywhere."

Father Uhtred, who was looking rather anxious, said, "Forgive me, my lords, but might it not be better to come and speak more privately? I would certainly like to think you are safe here, but in these sorry times, who can tell? Even the walls have ears…"

"But surely not the hawthorn tree?" whispered Math to Fleda, who was rather shocked at his lack of respect for the holy thorn.

They were taken to the abbot's quarters, and there they met Herefyrth, the abbot. Unlike Uhtred, his monk's habit hung loosely from a gaunt frame. His back was stooped from praying. His head was held slightly to

189

one side, as if he was more used to listening than talking. His expression was mild, but all the same, Fleda felt shy with him. He looked deep into her eyes, and she had the feeling he could read her thoughts.

When Alfred asked him for his blessing, he nodded quietly. "I would gladly bring our whole community together to offer up our prayers, but from what Aethelnoth tells me, you have need of secrecy, and so only Uhtred and I know the truth of who you are. I shall withdraw now, and spend the time until you leave in prayer for you. Yours is a great burden. I will ask God to give you the strength you need to bear it."

"Thank you, Your Grace," said Alfred quietly.

The abbot's dark eyes rested a little longer on Alfred. Then he excused himself, leaving them in Uhtred's hands.

While Herefyrth looked to their souls, Uhtred concerned himself with their bodies, eager to ply them with the best the abbey could offer. But Alfred wasn't interested in the wine from Francia, or the fish from the abbot's fishpond, or the fresh warm bread made from flour grown on abbey lands and milled and stored in its granaries. He leant forward, and said to Aethelnoth, "Now. Tell us what you know. Where is Guthrum? What is he doing?"

"As far as I can tell you," Aethelnoth said, "Guthrum's base is at Chippenham. From there, he sends out raiding parties, to gather supplies for his army, to terrorize the people, and to plunder riches. He himself is constantly on the move, as I said: what drives him is his search for you.

"He roars through Wessex like a river in flood, destroying everything in his path. In particular, he has seized most of your halls and ransacked them. It's as if he wants to blot out any trace of you, and set himself where you should be."

Fleda flinched, but Alfred didn't notice. His face was fierce, and his eyes glinted with anger. But he said nothing, and Aethelnoth went on.

"Many of the Hampshire men we would have expected to fight have fled across the sea. As has Hereward."

"Hereward?" asked Math.

"The ealdorman of Wiltshire. He has a young wife and a fearful heart. But Swinlac has taken his place, and the people trust him. In Dorset..." He paused.

"Yes?" prompted Alfred.

Aethelnoth looked down at the table in front of him. "It is not clear what is happening in Dorset. But there are rumours that Guthrum has made some kind of a treaty there."

"With whom?" asked Alfred.

"With your nephew, my lord – with Aethelwold."

Alfred sat silent and still for a moment. Nobody said a word. At last he looked up.

"Is that all?"

"I'm afraid not." Aethelnoth took a deep breath, and went on. "There is another Viking force – over a thousand men. They are in southern Wales at the moment, and it looks as if they are preparing themselves for an attack on the Devon coast. But Odda, the ealdorman of Devon, is ready for them. They will not have an easy fight on their hands. It seems likely that their hope was – is – to trap you between the two forces."

"They probably think they hardly need to bother now," said Alfred, "but you see, Aethelnoth – they're wrong. Quite wrong. Now, you've told me all the bad news – at least I hope you have. Do you have anything good to tell us?"

Aethelnoth smiled. "Undoubtedly the best news is that you are still alive, my lord. Other than that – we cannot count on Dorset, that's clear. The men of Devon will have their hands full. That leaves those that remain of the men of Hampshire, which is most of them – only the wealthiest were able to abandon their homes and pay for passage abroad; the men of Wiltshire under Swinlac, and the men of Somerset."

"And if I call on them, will they come?" asked Alfred.

Aethelnoth hesitated. "I think that many of them would come without question. But ... people talk. They hear stories, and the stories get more frightening as they pass from mouth to mouth. There are those who believe now that nothing can stop the Danes. There have been so many battles over the last few years ... the people need to be convinced, my lord."

Alfred nodded. "Others have said this too." He glanced at Math, who bowed slightly.

Aethelnoth hadn't finished. "You should also be aware, my lord, that there are those who hold a finger to the wind to see which way it blows. And if they sense that it is blowing in the Danes' favour, they will swiftly change sides."

"Such as my nephew," said Alfred briefly.

"Yes. But there will be others, less easily recognized. We must be wary."

Aethelnoth suggested that the best way to influence the largest number of people was to go to the hundred courts. Each shire was divided into hundreds, and each hundred held a meeting once a month to settle any problems or disputes that had arisen. Oswald frowned.

"But great heavens, man, there are hundreds of hundreds. How can we possibly get round them all?"

"It isn't difficult," said Aethelnoth. "If I wish to get a message to all the hundreds, I use the shire assemblies if possible, because representatives from the hundreds come there. But they're only twice a year, even in times of peace. At the moment I'd be wary of holding one for fear of attracting Guthrum – it would be a good opportunity for him to destroy the most powerful men in Somerset in one fell swoop.

"But there is another way. It's like spiders' webs. At the centre of each web is a certain hundred. That one will send messages to others surrounding it. So we need not send a messenger to all of them. And the ealdormen of the other shires will be able to do the same."

Alfred sat back, and looked round at all of them. "How long? How long before we can gather our largest force together?"

"Some weeks, my lord."

"Which will bring you close to the sowing season," added Math. "There'll be no victory for anyone if there isn't enough grain to feed the people afterwards."

Oswald looked impatient, but Alfred nodded. "You're right to remind us of it, Math. So — we're looking towards a month after Easter, maybe even a little more." He drummed his fingers on the surface of the table, and his eyes narrowed thoughtfully. "The gathering point for the men of Somerset will be Athelney. The island has defences now, and as men arrive, they can build more huts. It will give Björn and Ulric the time they need to make more weapons — and there will be other smiths to join them. But the earliest arrivals — they will need more than carpentry and building work to keep them occupied. And as several of you have said — the people need to know that there is hope. We need some triumphs, and we will also need food for the army as it grows. Who better to take it from than the Danes?" His eyes sparkled, and his smile was infectious.

"Aethelnoth, Math. Can you find me a core of men — fifty, say, to start off with? It's time we started to get our own back. The Northmen have been having it their way for far too long..."

And so the main business of their meeting was concluded. But as they rose, ready now for the food Uhtred had offered them earlier, Aethelnoth hesitated.

"I heard a strange story. I don't know what to make of it, but it may interest you.

"It concerns Markham Priory in Wiltshire. It received a visit from Guthrum a couple of weeks ago. The monks had warning, and they had time to escape. But the prior, Matthew, refused to leave, or even to hide himself. Apparently he waited for Guthrum at the altar of the church."

Alfred raised his eyebrows. "Brave, but foolish," he said.

"Yes. But then something strange happened. Guthrum ordered his men to kill Matthew, as you would expect. But Matthew requested that if he was to be killed, it should be by Guthrum himself. And Guthrum changed his mind. I don't know why – I haven't met this Matthew myself. Anyway, whatever the reason for it, though he still allowed his men to destroy as much as they wanted of the priory, Guthrum ordered them not to lay a finger on Matthew himself. Which seemed to me curious."

Alfred looked interested. "Perhaps I should speak to Matthew. He seems to hold the key to Guthrum's heart!"

Oswald grunted. "The only key we need to Guthrum's

heart is a very sharp knife. If he has a heart at all, which I doubt…"

Something had been worrying Fleda: something that Aethelnoth had mentioned quite early on. She took a deep breath, and spoke up.

"My lord," she said. "You said that Guthrum has seized many of my father's halls. I – I was wondering – did he … is Winchester one of them?"

Aethelnoth looked surprised, and glanced at Alfred for an explanation.

"Forgive me, Aethelnoth – this is my daughter, the Princess Aethelfled."

Aethelnoth's face cleared, and he turned back to Fleda. "I see – I'm sorry, my lady, I didn't know. In answer to your question… " He glanced at Alfred, as if he was asking permission to go on, and Alfred nodded, looking tense as he waited for Aethelnoth to continue.

"In answer to your question – yes, Guthrum has taken Winchester."

Fleda hardly noticed as Alfred murmured to the others that they should go on to the refectory, and he would follow. She felt cold.

She seemed to hear Edward's voice, as if from a long distance, bubbling over with enthusiasm as he told her about the dam he and his friend Sebbi had made at Winchester. She remembered how she had persuaded him to get ready to go, and how she had watched, hidden, as her mother, Edward, and her little sisters had ridden off into the night. To Winchester – to safety.

"I never said goodbye to Mother," she whispered. "The last thing I did was to trick her."

Alfred crouched down and took her by the shoulders. "It's all right. Fleda, it's all right. I… "

For a moment, he was quiet. Then he said gently, "I sent them to safety. Not to the palace, and not to Winchester itself. To a farmstead a few miles outside, in a valley that's well hidden and easily defended. And I sent them with Britnoth, whom I would trust with my life."

"Then they're safe?" she said eagerly. "Are you sure?"

He hesitated. "I wish I could say so for certain. They are as safe as I was able to make them. I did the best that I could."

Fleda listened in dismay. It was a bitter shock to realize that her father's best might not be good enough.

"Then what shall we do?" she demanded. "Can we go to Winchester and find them?"

He looked away from her, so that she could only see his face in profile, a sharp, angular outline that could have been carved from rock.

"No," he said. "We cannot."

She knew that voice. It was final.

She stared at the peaceful grounds round the abbey. Snowdrops grew among the grass, and birds were singing, as though everything was all right in the world. But it wasn't. She turned away from her father, her mouth set in a furious line. He didn't care about her mother, he didn't care about any of them. All he cared about was Wessex and the stupid Danes. Her face felt hot and angry and her eyes were smarting, but she held her head high so that the tears wouldn't be able to fall, and she began to walk away.

"I don't want any food," she said over her shoulder, her voice thin and cold. She didn't look back, so she didn't see the pain in her father's face.

It was a long time before she fell asleep that night. In the bare little room, she lay on a hard bed like the ones the monks slept in, and tried to remember what Sebbi looked like. It upset her more than anything that she couldn't remember his face. He was just a little boy who liked to play in the mud and build dams. She hoped he'd found somewhere to hide when the Vikings came.

She couldn't hold back the tears now. They welled out of her eyes and trickled across her cheeks, warm and salty.

Treachery and Trickery

GUTHRUM STARED AT THE MONK grovelling in front of him. All you have to do, he thought, is find a man with a grudge – the right man – and he'll tell you all you need to know. This one hated the abbot of Glastonbury for such a ridiculous reason Guthrum couldn't even remember what it was. It was Snorri who'd sniffed him out. He was good at that kind of thing, Snorri. A nasty, shifty-eyed little man – not much of a fighter, but he could always be relied on to pick out the rotten apple in the barrel. Oh yes – that was it: the monk hated the abbot because he'd put an end to some nice little scam involving the sale of the fruit and vegetables grown in the abbey garden.

Guthrum touched the monk with his foot.

"Come on then," he said. "What have you got to tell me? What have you seen? It'd better be good, I warn you. I really don't like being disturbed when I'm in the middle of a meal."

The monk swallowed, and tried unsuccessfully to return Guthrum's cold stare. There was a scar on the Danish leader's cheek, and the monk wondered fleetingly what had happened to the man who'd put it there. Guthrum leant towards him.

"I'm waiting," he said softly, "but not for much longer."

The monk found his voice.

"Strangers," he croaked. "Strangers came to the abbey. Three men and a boy. And the ealdorman, Aethelnoth, came to meet them — I knew him, I've seen him before."

"And?" prompted Guthrum.

"Aethelnoth bent his knee to one of the men. Why would he do that? Who would an ealdorman kneel to — if not the king?"

Guthrum felt a stirring of excitement inside his chest.

"What did he look like, this other man?"

"He had his hood pulled down over his face. But he was tall, almost as tall as you, my lord."

"There are many tall men, even among this miserable nation of yours."

"Yes, but also, he stretched out his hand when Aethelnoth knelt."

It had been a fine hand, long fingered and shapely. But the monk knew that Guthrum wouldn't want to hear that, so he went on. "He was wearing a ring. I wasn't close, but the sun glinted on it. It was gold right enough, and it was huge. It was in the shape of some sort of animal, I think — a dragon, perhaps. I've never seen a ring like it."

"But I have," murmured Guthrum, clenching his fist. "I've seen it many times. The dragon of Wessex!" He stood up so abruptly that he knocked his chair over. "It was him — it was Alfred! It must have been!"

He had been striding restlessly back and forth across the room, but suddenly he swung round, marched over to the unfortunate monk, and seized him by the throat.

"How long ago?" he demanded.

"Earlier today, my lord."

Guthrum threw back his head and howled. "Then we've lost him! Why didn't you get here faster, fool?"

The monk cowered. "Forgive me, my lord – I did the best I could. I had to have a reason to leave, so I offered to go to the fish house at Meare, but I couldn't do that straight away. And, and, I don't think you have lost him, because I heard it said that they were staying overnight..."

"Hmm. Then we may still catch him. And if we don't, your abbot's going to be sorry he was so hospitable. Ivar, Thorkil, spread the word – we ride at first light." As they left the room, he turned back to the monk and bared his teeth in a grin. "You'll be wanting a reward, I suppose. Don't worry, I'll see that you get one."

As he left the room, he said casually to Ragnar, who stood by the door, "Kill him. He'll be no more use to us, and I don't like traitors."

Fleda didn't want to speak to her father or even to look at him. It was easy enough to avoid him. He was very much in demand; everyone seemed to have something to say to him before they left the next morning. The abbot took them into the great church to give Alfred his formal blessing before the altar. Herefyrth stood in front, with one hand resting lightly on an ornate golden casket, gesturing towards it with the other.

"This reliquary contains a piece of the staff that St Patrick took with him when he went to do God's work in Ireland. You may know that he spent many years at this

201

abbey before he left to do his great work. Like you, he had to wrestle with the heathens for their souls; he had to fight many demons. I ask him to intercede with Our Lord, so that He may guide and protect you in the great task that lies ahead, and give you no burden which you are unable to bear."

His eyes rested gravely on Alfred as he made the sign of the cross over him, and they alighted on Fleda too, with an expression of great gentleness. Alfred stood up. He looked relaxed and calm, and he held his hand out to help her up. But she ignored it, and failed to notice Herefyrth's concerned glance, locked as she was in her grief and anger.

It was time to go. Aethelnoth clasped hands with Alfred, and they spoke quietly together. But Fleda didn't listen. She wasn't interested, and she hardly even managed to thank kindly Uhtred when he shyly presented her with some oatcakes sweetened with honey.

It was a relief to see Cerys, who was waiting for them at the boats by the shore of the lake, but she seemed to be wrapped in her own thoughts. The early morning mist clung to the water. Fleda felt quite alone, lost in a featureless white world with no sense of direction.

After a time, she looked up to see Cerys's gaze fixed on her.

"Something has happened," said Cerys. "Would you like to talk about it?"

And Fleda felt the tight knot inside her chest begin to

loosen, just a little, as she told Cerys about her fears and her anger with her father.

Cerys listened very carefully. Then she said, "If I were your father, I would probably have taken a horse and ridden straight off to Winchester. And what would have happened then?"

Fleda stared at her, but said nothing.

"I might not ever have reached Winchester – that's the first thing. We don't know where Guthrum is, or even if all of his men are together. There may be raiders anywhere, all of them longing to be the ones to find your father. And then Wessex would be without a king. Or, I might reach Winchester to find your mother and family safe, in which case I would have wasted my time. Or, I might find that they had already left – gone to Francia, perhaps. Or ... " She paused. "Or, if the worst happened, I might find that I had arrived too late, and they were already dead. Think about it. Without an army, what could I do then, that wouldn't end in my death and the end of Wessex?

"He's not just a father, Fleda. He's a king, and he has to think about what comes first. And at the moment, it's driving the Danes back. That's first, last, and what's in the middle as well. Nothing else matters."

The men had waited till they were in sight of the shore, and then gone ahead up the hill. Cerys and Fleda followed more slowly, and a wide gap opened up between them.

When they reached the top, they stopped a while to catch their breath, and looked back to see where they had come from. The mist had cleared, and the water lay silk smooth in the sunshine.

Suddenly Cerys stiffened.

"I can hear something," she said.

Faint cries and shouts carried across the lake.

"What's that?" said Fleda. Although the cries were distant, it was impossible not to hear the note of terror in them, and she felt a surge of fear which filled her chest and pushed up into her throat, so that she could hardly breathe. She looked at Cerys, her eyes asking a question.

Cerys stood very still, straining to see and hear.

"There's smoke," she said. "It's coming from the abbey."

Fleda swallowed. "It's them, isn't it?" she demanded. "It's the Danes." A new, terrible thought struck her. "They must have known my father was there! They came to look for him – they're there because of him!"

"Fleda…"

But Fleda wasn't listening. She had shouldered the punt and was already slipping and slithering back down the hill.

"NO!" cried Cerys. "What are you doing? Come back!"

Fleda turned and shouted furiously, "No! I'm going back there! It's our fault, and I'm not running away!"

Cerys looked desperately in the direction where Math, Alfred and Oswald had gone, but she couldn't see them – that side of the hill was thickly wooded. She shouted to them, but no one answered, and she knew that if she waited any longer, Fleda would reach the shore. It was madness, but there was no choice. She had to follow. She plunged down the hill after the girl.

Fleda was perfectly clear. She was going to go back to Glastonbury. She wasn't stupid, she didn't intend to march into the middle of whatever was happening, she would wait until it was safe – but the one thing she wasn't going to do was run away to safety.

"They are there because of my father," she told Cerys defiantly. "They must have heard he was there – someone must have betrayed him. So it's our fault! I'll wait till they've gone, but then I need to see. I need to see for myself what they do. I need to see if I can help."

She was so small, Cerys thought. She was just a child. But her face was fierce, and the line of her chin was as firm as her father's. She would not change her mind. Cerys closed her eyes for a moment, thinking.

"Very well," she said curtly. "We will keep close to the shore until we reach the side of the tor away from the town. Then we'll climb it, and we'll be able to look down and see what's happening. I will try to keep you safe. But you must do exactly as I say. Is it agreed?"

There was a long moment, and then Fleda nodded stiffly.

Once in the boat, Cerys sat still as a statue. Only her lips moved, to form words that Fleda didn't recognize.

Her voice was soft and musical and persuasive, and Fleda found that her eyelids were growing heavy. Why, Cerys was trying to trick her, to send her to sleep! She shook her head and blinked, but just as she was about to accuse her, she noticed that mist was forming again, curling round the boat, spreading along the shores of the lake, forming a thick veil behind which they could move unseen. And she remembered Alfred's story of the first time he had seen Cerys, long ago, when he was hunting.

She wondered if he had realized yet that she and Cerys were no longer following them. Perhaps he had climbed back up the hill to look for them, and seen the smoke and heard the shouts, as they had. He would be worried...

She pushed the thought away, and held onto the anger.

They were almost at the top of the tor. It was a hard climb; the tor was steep, and because they wanted to keep on the side away from the town and the abbey, they were climbing more or less straight up.

The mist had thinned and drifted away; Cerys said briefly that they would be safe on the hill. When they reached the top, lying flat on their stomachs so that they couldn't be seen from below, they had a clear view of the abbey grounds, which only that morning had looked so serene and well ordered.

* * *

Some of Guthrum's men had peeled off into Glastonbury itself to make sure that the townspeople were too busy saving themselves to come to the aid of the abbey. They didn't try too hard: if people had sensibly shut themselves inside their houses and closed their eyes and ears to what might be happening to anyone else, the Danes were content to leave them there. They amused themselves by riding among the market stalls and trampling on what they didn't want, occasionally scooping up a desirable trinket on the point of a sword, casually slaughtering anyone who gave the slightest sign of resistance.

The real target was the abbey. The monks were going about their daily work when the Danes swept into the town from the east. Those working in the vegetable garden were the first to hear the relentless thud of the Northmen's hooves; they were glad of the excuse to straighten their stiff backs and look round to see who these latest visitors were.

It was probably their cries that alerted the more learned brothers working industriously at their books in the scriptorium. Those working in the kitchen heard nothing over the crackling of the fire, the sizzling of pots and the clatter of pans; or maybe they did, and made a desperate attempt to hide in the cellars. If so, it did them no good. The Danes were very thorough, and few of the monks escaped Guthrum's anger when he realized that Alfred had eluded him again.

Not all the brothers were old or weak or particularly

gentle – far from it. Given the chance, most of them would have grabbed a staff, a spade, a knife – anything that came to hand – and defended themselves.

But they didn't have that chance. By the time they knew their death was approaching, it was upon them. When Cerys and Fleda had reached the top of the tor and were peering down into the abbey grounds, it was all over, and there was nothing much to see.

Just small scattered figures, easily recognized by their dark robes, crumpled like heaps of rags on the ground. Moving among them were men with helmets and weapons in their hands, striding in and out of the great church, the smaller lady chapel, the cloisters, the dormitory, clearly searching for something or someone. And in the open, close to a small twisted black tree, which Fleda knew must be Joseph of Arimathea's thorn, a figure sat hunched and still on a great horse. Fleda wondered, with a stab of fear, if it was Guthrum himself.

Many of the Danes emerged from the buildings with their arms full. Some of what they were carrying went straight onto a bonfire, but what they considered worth saving was piled onto a cart that the Danes had prudently brought with them.

Finally, the activity slowed. The Danes gathered together round their leader. Fleda and Cerys saw Guthrum raise his arm in command. One of the men plunged something into the bonfire, which was burning with a merry crackle that carried through the still air. He took the resultant torch over to a building near the kitchen.

"What's that building?" said Cerys.

"I think it's the granary," said Fleda, her throat dry.

"No! Surely they're not—"

But they were. They couldn't carry so much grain away, and they didn't want to leave it for anyone else. So they burned it. And as the hungry flames caught hold and created an inferno that could be seen for almost as far as the tor itself, the Danes let out a ragged cheer.

It was a small triumph but not the one they'd wanted. Guthrum had already turned his back on the abbey and was riding away, and his men followed him, leaving the people of Glastonbury to emerge from their houses and bury their dead.

It hadn't taken long for Alfred, Math and Oswald to realize that Cerys and Fleda were no longer following them. Puzzled, they went back up the hill.

"Look," said Oswald. "There are footprints here. They came to the top, and then one of them went back down. It must have been the princess: the prints are smaller. Here, she slid in the mud ... and Cerys followed her. It looks as if they both went back down to the shore."

Alfred looked up sharply. "Do you hear that?"

The cries and screams, echoing across the gently lapping water...

He and Oswald stared at each other, their eyes

mirroring each other's dread. They'd heard such sounds many times before.

"It must be one of Guthrum's raiding parties," said Oswald. "Looking for you, like Aethelnoth said."

"Are you sure?" asked Math, disbelieving. "How can you tell?"

"What else could it be?" said Oswald tersely. "People are screaming! Someone's been telling tales. We weren't secret enough."

Math opened his mouth to speak, but Alfred cut in.

"What does this mean? *Where is my daughter?*"

Recognizing the anguish in his voice, Math said quickly, "We'll find her! We will find her!" And he looked round, his eyes sharp as an eagle, his gaze darting all over the lake. Then he stiffened, and pointed. "There. Do you see that mist? Just by the edge of the lake?"

"What witchery is this?" gasped Oswald. "One patch of fog on the whole lake? See how it moves! That isn't ordinary fog!"

"Cerys," said Math briefly. "It has to be. You know she has certain skills."

"So you say. And so we've seen. But tell me this, British man. If that is indeed Cerys, what is she doing taking the princess back to Glastonbury?"

Oswald's voice was menacing, but Alfred put a hand on his shoulder. "Think, Oswald. Fleda went first. Her footprints were ahead of Cerys's. It was she who led the way." He moved away a little, and stared across the

210

water, creasing his eyes as if he would see what was happening there. "But why? Could there have been something she'd forgotten, some reason she had for wanting to go back to the abbey? Or did they hear the screams, as we did? Is *that* why she went back?"

Oswald frowned. "Surely, if they thought the Danes were there, that would be as good a reason as any for running very fast in the opposite direction!"

Alfred sighed. "She's angry with me. She has a big heart, and she's stubborn. Who knows what she expected to achieve? Perhaps she's going to take on the Danes all by herself. We have to go after them."

"I'm not my sister," warned Math. "I can't summon fog for us to hide behind."

"No," said Alfred tersely. "We'll just have to keep close into the shore and hope that the Danes are too busy to notice us. Come on."

Fleda lay still, staring down at the abbey numbly. It would be safe to go down now, she knew that. But she found she wanted to keep a distance between herself and the horrors down there on the soft emerald grass.

"Can we go now?" she said to Cerys, her voice trembling slightly.

"No, we can't. At least I can't, not now that I've seen what's happened. And you're safer with me than without me, so you must come too. There's no danger now. The Vikings have gone, you saw that." There was an edge to

Cerys's voice, and Fleda turned to look at her, but Cerys avoided her eyes and just dashed a hand across her cheek impatiently. "I've never had much time for the priests, nor they for me, but to see them cut down like that... Perhaps we'll find one alive. There's been too much death already today. I'll do what I can to make sure there's no more." And she was off, striding down the hill. Fleda had little choice but to follow her and, feeling troubled and vaguely ashamed, she did so.

The first one she saw was Uhtred. He was lying on his back. His head had fallen back at a peculiar angle, and as she knelt down beside him, she saw why. Someone had cut his throat. It was a deep, gaping cut, and she found herself thinking, stupidly, it was a good job it wasn't summer, or the flies would be clustering round it.

She could imagine the scene. Gates bursting open and poor Uhtred stepping back in horror, and one of them grabbing him from behind. He would have felt the sharp steel point against his throat. She remembered his kindness to her that morning, when he'd given her bread for the journey; she'd been so full of anger towards her father that she'd barely bothered to thank him. She felt anger again now, but it was a different kind of anger, slow burning but focused, implacable, and it had a different target.

Uhtred's dark robes were rucked up above his knees. She straightened them, and then hesitated. His eyes

212

stared up at the sky, reflecting the light of the last day he'd seen. She should try to shut them, she thought, and she stretched out her fingers but couldn't bring herself to do it. What if they wouldn't close? She touched his cheek instead. It was still warm.

Everywhere she looked, there was death. It had caught up with the monks in the vegetable garden; one of them must have held up his arms to defend himself, because they were hacked almost to pieces. Another had tried to run and received a savage wound in his back, falling across the earth he'd been digging, for sowing seed in the spring. It was more than she could bear. A sob rose in her throat, and hot tears flooded her eyes.

Suddenly someone grasped her shoulders and terror engulfed her. Her body hunched, her hands went up to protect her face and she screamed, a thin wail of paralyzing fear. Then she was being held close in tender arms, and breathing in her father's familiar smell, of wool and warmth and leather. Here was her father, here was safety.

She stood up, shakily at first, and looked round slowly, sparing herself nothing. "They didn't have a chance," she said softly. "Not a chance."

Before he could answer, they heard Cerys calling urgently from inside the great church.

She was in front of the high altar, cradling the head of someone who lay sprawled across the steps. It was the abbot, Herefyrth.

"He's alive," she said quietly, "but only just."

There was a large patch of blood on the front of his robe, and another on the side of his head. His skin, already pale before, had the colour and texture of candle wax. His dark eyes, dim with pain, found Alfred's face, and a small light came into them. Alfred kneeled beside him.

"Who was it?"

"Guthrum…" The word came out like a long sigh. "He took … the reliquary … and the cross," he whispered. "I tried … to stop him, but he … used the cross … to strike me."

Fleda gasped in horror, and her father's face tightened with anger.

Herefyrth closed his eyes for a moment, and he drew a shuddering breath.

Alfred leant over him and grabbed his hands. "I will kill him," he said fiercely, "you have my word on it, and the cross will be restored."

The abbot moved his head slightly, shaking it. His eyes burned into Alfred's. "Don't … kill. Always … too much killing… But the reliquary … must return. It belongs … here. Our dearest … treasure."

"You don't want me to kill Guthrum? Even after all this?" Alfred's voice was disbelieving.

They could see that Herefyrth had to summon all his strength just to speak.

"Christ … teaches us … to forgive. We must … try. Or … no better … than them."

Alfred hesitated for only a moment. Then he nodded. "It shall be as you wish. I swear it."

The abbot closed his eyes for a moment, and his forehead creased in pain. Cerys smoothed it with her long fingers, and she murmured something so softly that none of the others could hear her words. Herefyrth opened his eyes again, eager and hopeful, looking up into her face as if it was the face of his mother. His lips moved, but all that emerged was a low, whistling sigh. It was his last breath.

Few of the monks were left to bury their dead, but soon, people from the town began to emerge from their hiding places and cautiously came to the abbey to see what had happened. The fire in the granary had blazed fiercely; the grain was all gone, the roof a stark tracery of smouldering black timbers. The stench of smoke and death hung over the scene like a pall, and at first the people could do nothing but stand and gaze around them in bewilderment. Some felt ashamed that they had done nothing to help. One man stirred the ashes at the edge of the smaller bonfire with his foot.

"What could we have done?" he said to no one in particular. "We weren't ready. Why didn't anybody warn us?"

"Who?" said another angrily. "There is nobody. No one who cares about the likes of us, anyway."

"There's no point in that sort of talk," said a third man briefly. "Come on. There's work to do."

"The reeve," murmured Math to Alfred. "Oswyn. He's a good man. Not much imagination, a bit slow, but thorough."

"Then let's leave him to bury the dead," said Alfred crisply. "I made a promise and I'm going to keep it. Math, you know Oswyn. Can you get him to provide us with horses? We must follow the Danes, and quickly, or we'll lose them. I want to catch them before they rejoin the main army."

Oswald's eyes widened. He looked round at Math, Cerys and Fleda, and then back at Alfred.

"Follow them?" he said incredulously. "With three men, a woman and a child? What good will that do?"

"When the woman is Cerys, the child is my daughter, and the men are you, Math, and the king of Wessex, a great deal of good. We're going to send out a message. I'm back and, soon, I'll want everyone to know it. Math, the horses, please. Tell Oswyn whatever you have to, but as yet, don't say who I am. Oswald, go with him. Cerys, a word…"

The instinct to obey was clearly struggling in Oswald with the conviction that Alfred had taken leave of his senses. He glanced at Fleda, his forehead furrowed with anxiety.

"But, my lord, is this wise? Think of your daughter!"

Alfred hesitated, and looked at Fleda. "Perhaps Oswald is right. Perhaps you should wait here."

Fleda shook her head. "I don't want to be left behind,"

she said with determination. "And anyway…" What she wanted to say was that she trusted her father to keep her safe, or as safe as anyone could. But that was too dificult to say in front of other people. "Anyway," she said, "it's not going to be a battle, is it? What you need is a trick. And I'm good at tricks."

Cerys smiled. "So am I," she murmured.

Oswald glared at her. "Well, I know that!" he said, and stomped off with Math to find horses, muttering crossly.

The horses Oswyn found for them were strong and sturdy. It was a pity they weren't built for speed, but these were working horses, and they were the best that could be found. Word got round that gold coins had changed hands, and there were some curious looks as the strangers rode off in the same direction the Northmen had taken. But all Oswyn could say was that they were men of quality, or so he judged by their clothes and their weapons. He stood looking after them, shaking his head.

"We won't be seeing them again, you mark my words. Be more sense in it if they were riding the other way…"

Guthrum was bitterly disappointed. He had been so close, so near to finishing it. If the monk had been right – and he felt sure from all he'd heard that he had been – Alfred had been in the abbey with only a few men, if any, to protect him. He could have been captured – and not only that, he could have been totally humiliated before being despatched in a way that would have sent a clear message throughout the Isles of Britain and beyond – the blood eagle perhaps, or a variation of it. There was no one else, no one left who mattered. With him finally out of the way, Guthrum would have reigned supreme.

He still would, of course. It was only a matter of time. Alfred had no means of fighting back. If he had, he would have shown himself by now – he wouldn't be skulking about in woods or caves or swamps, or wherever it was that he'd managed to conceal himself.

But, though Guthrum would hardly admit it to himself, let alone anyone else, he was beginning to feel he'd had enough of fighting, of being always on the move from one battle to the next. It was years since he'd first left Denmark. His elder brother had taken over their father's farm – that was all right: Nils had a family, children, and anyway he liked farming. He didn't have that pale blue gaze that Guthrum had, that way of scanning the horizon, always looking for somewhere new, somewhere better, somewhere with more space. Nils's blood didn't surge when he heard the lonely, mewling cry of a seagull, and watched its effortless, reeling flight across a huge and empty sky, not the way Guthrum's did.

So Guthrum had left, first on someone else's boat, then on his own. He'd used the sea as a road, the rivers as paths to riches and greatness, penetrating into the heart of one soft, wealthy country after another.

But now his beard was threaded with silver and his old wounds ached when it was damp, and he found that after all, he had a wish to settle down, to find a wife and breed children to carry on his name. King Guthrum … why not? This island country would suit him well. Surrounded by his old ally the sea, it would be easy to defend from other adventurers. There was plenty of good, fertile land, and there were riches to take and to build on. He'd got the rest of it already; only Wessex was holding out, and Wessex was an apple, waiting to fall.

But not while Alfred was still out there somewhere. Because he was an enemy to reckon with, Guthrum knew that. He was down and very nearly out, but until Guthrum actually saw his head on a platter, he knew he could not discount him. In the last two years, since Guthrum had first arrived, they'd fought a string of battles on sea and on land; they'd chased each other the length and breadth of Wessex and back again. But in his heart of hearts, Guthrum had to admit that, for the most part, Alfred had had the better of him. The Englishman's only weakness was his faith in other people. He thought that just because he believed in promises, everyone else did too. A big mistake, and one that Guthrum was only too happy to exploit. He'd broken every treaty they'd ever made, even when it meant abandoning hostages to whatever might be their fate, as he had at Wareham and then again at Exeter. He'd sworn by his own gods and by Alfred's, and noticed with interest that nothing much seemed to happen when he broke his word.

He had to find him. He would return to Chippenham and collect more men – he'd smother Somerset with spies and in the end, he would smoke Alfred out.

They had reached the edge of the plain. Chippenham was to the north, and that was where he'd intended to go till he'd heard the monk's tale. What a waste of effort ... still, he had always meant to turn his attention to Glastonbury sooner or later. He looked with some satisfaction at the cart, which contained silver altar plates, books with ornate jewelled covers and glittering robes, barrels of beer, sacks of flour, tubs of saltfish and rounds of cheese. It wasn't what he'd wanted, but it was better than nothing.

It had been a long ride and a tiring day, but soon they'd be back at the manor house they'd left that morning. He was looking forward to the beer: he didn't feel much like feasting, but the idea of drowning his sorrows had a good deal of appeal.

It was so lonely being a leader. You had to keep everybody scared; you had to have respect, else you wouldn't last five minutes. But just sometimes, it would be so nice to have someone to talk to – someone to comfort you and tell you everything would be all right.

He jerked upright in the saddle and glared round, as if he thought someone might have overheard his thoughts. What was this creeping weakness? He'd never been in the habit of wasting energy thinking and feeling, and this was certainly not the time to start.

The sun was about to set. Gold-edged grey clouds billowed against a deep blue sky. It would be a cold night. Another good reason for drinking.

He wondered if Alfred was watching the sunset, and if so, where from. He hoped he'd heard about the abbey. If he knew Alfred, it would upset him, make him angry. He didn't like it when anyone slighted his god. Guthrum smiled. He hoped Alfred would be cold this night, cold and very miserable.

"Soon, Alfred," he muttered. "Soon."

It hadn't been difficult to follow the Danes – they were a large group of men and, as far as they knew, there was no reason to hide their trail. They were arrogant, Alfred thought. Arrogance would make them careless, and that would give him his chance.

"They've stopped," said Math softly.

The road ran alongside a ridge that rose up to the right. To the left, there was a large farm, nestling at the foot of a gentle slope and facing the much steeper ridge. It was a pleasant-looking place with its deep thatched roof and neat orchard to one side. Fleda hoped its rightful owners hadn't shared the same fate as Ulric's family. Surely the Danes couldn't keep on killing at this rate? Who would look after the animals and take care of the land if they did?

The Danish force had ridden into the yard and were dismounting, leading their horses into an enclosure and the cart into a barn, and then going in ones and twos into the house.

"Look!" said Cerys.

She was pointing up at the ridge. There, gleaming silver in the last rays of the sun, was the figure of a white horse cut into the hillside, the curved lines of its neck and hind legs sharp and powerful.

"Oh!" said Fleda in delight. "It's lovely! Why is it there?"

"I don't know," admitted Alfred. "But it's not the first one I've seen. There's another one a long way from here, not far from Wantage, at Ashdown."

"Now there was a battle!" said Oswald. "We had them on the run that time!"

Alfred grinned, remembering how Redi had insisted

221

on finishing his prayers, and Alfred had lost patience and started the battle without him. But his smile faded as he remembered that though they'd won that battle, they'd lost the next one. And soon after that, Guthrum had arrived and Redi had died.

"Is the other horse the same, Father?"

He realized they were all looking at him, and he came quickly back to the present. "It's similar. Bigger, I think. And less like a real horse. Just curved lines, really. The way a child might draw a horse, perhaps."

Cerys was looking thoughtfully up at the horse. "But it wasn't made by children. It was made by people long ago – my people, perhaps – as was this one – though I think this is more recent. They were offerings to the gods: they are things of power." She turned to Alfred. "I think I have an idea…"

Guthrum was feeling much better. At least, he thought he was. He wasn't completely sure, because everything had become pleasantly fuzzy. The monks' ale was certainly very good. In fact, he thought blearily, it was a pity he'd had them all killed. He should have kept some of them, then they could have brewed beer for him … he'd always had a quick temper, he thought sadly. It was all Alfred's fault. Everything was Alfred's fault…

He blinked. He'd been staring into the fire, which was in the centre of the room. The flames were leaping higher and higher; the way they were weaving round each other, you'd almost think they were dancing in time to the music.

Music? Now, where had that come from? He peered through the flames, trying to puzzle it out. Last time he'd heard a sound like that, he'd been a little boy, listening to a skald in a chieftain's hall telling stories of heroes and gods and monsters. The skald had accompanied his stories with a harp; it had been such a sweet sound ... and so was this.

But he could hardly hear it through the noise the men were making. They were bragging and telling jokes and guffawing with laughter, getting louder and louder as they had to shout to make themselves heard. Impatiently, he stood up and pushed the table over, so that it crashed onto the floor. That shut them up all right. He glared round at them.

"Hush!" he said fiercely, and put a finger to his lips. "Listen!"

The notes from the harp dropped into the silence like golden honey, smooth and sweet. The men had looked annoyed at being interrupted in their merrymaking, but as they heard the music, some began to glance round, fearful and puzzled; some, suspicious and hostile, fingered their knives — but most just listened intently, their faces touched with wonder.

"It's coming from outside," whispered Ivar.

"I don't care where it's coming from," snapped Guthrum. "I like it, and I want to be able to listen to it!"

For a few moments, they were silent, some of them swaying gently in time to the music. But then Guthrum realized that his ears were straining — the music was growing fainter. "Quick!" he said. "Outside — after it! Find out who's playing and let's have them in!"

But they were all too full of beer to do anything quickly. They stumbled and fell over each other as they crowded through the doorway, and by the time they'd sorted themselves out and picked themselves up, the lilting, magical music was dancing away into the distance.

"After it!" roared Guthrum, his great arm extended, pointing up towards the ridge, which was where the sound seemed to be heading. "Fetch me that harpist!"

Cheering lustily, the pack set off. Only Ragnar, who never drank, stood staring after them, his eyebrows drawn together in a suspicious scowl. But then he shrugged his shoulders and decided after all that he might as well follow them.

And it was as well he did. Otherwise, he might have seen the three figures, two tall and one much smaller, who slipped like shadows into the outbuilding where the treasure cart had been safely stowed. And he might have heard the cart creaking and the wheels rattling and the sound of hooves striking stone, as the thieves drove it swiftly west along the road, until all trace of it was lost in the night.

It was a merry chase at first, but the slope, gentle to begin with, soon became much steeper. The Danes' breathing became heavy and ragged, and one or two of them stumbled and decided on second thoughts that they didn't really care that much about the heavenly harpist any more, and they'd much rather curl up and go to sleep. But something about the music lured Guthrum on. He wanted it, and he was determined to have it.

"We're going towards the horse," said Thorkil.

Guthrum stopped, his chest heaving, and looked up. The white horse glittered strangely in the moonlight. He felt suddenly uneasy. He'd never seen anything like this before, but he vaguely sensed that it was old, and that it wasn't to do with ordinary mortal concerns. The

224

harp music lingered bewitchingly ahead of them, but he stood still, his eyes fixed uncertainly on the horse. He shook his head, wishing it felt clearer.

"What is it?" he whispered. "What is the horse?"

There was some pushing and shoving behind him, and he wheeled round, irritated.

"Well?" he demanded. "Anyone got anything to say?"

One of the men stumbled forward. "Ah ... there's this girl," he said unwillingly. There were cheers and hoots of laughter – until Guthrum's angry gaze blasted them all and allowed the man, Halfdan, to continue. "She's from the village, and – well, a few days ago we were up by the white horse." She had dark hair and flashing brown eyes and skin like cherries and cream, and Halfdan really liked her and thought she was the loveliest thing he'd ever seen, but he would never have dreamed of admitting such feelings to the others. "She told me that the horse belongs to a goddess, called Ep – Epona, I think it was. A goddess of war."

"Well then," said Ivar, "she should be on our side!"

Guthrum frowned. "Maybe," he muttered, "and maybe not."

Something was going to happen. He could feel it building. He looked round blearily and lifted his head, like a great stag sniffing the air.

Beside him, Thorkil gasped. "Look!"

At intervals round the outline of the horse, small fires were springing up, one by one. But they were no ordinary fires. The flames leaped up into slender columns of blazing white light, shot through with amethyst and emerald and sapphire, vivid against the deep dark blue of the night sky.

225

The men were brave enough to face any living enemy but this was something else altogether. It was only their fear of Guthrum that held them there, gazing fearfully at the white horse and its weird illumination. As the pillars of flame leaped higher and higher, the light became too dazzling, and few apart from Guthrum managed to keep watching.

But the next thing that happened was too much for everyone even, in the end, for Guthrum. The brightness confused their senses, but nevertheless all those who still had their eyes open were clear afterwards as to what happened next.

The horse, in a blur of misty movement, rose from the hillside onto its feet, so that it stood before them alive and restless, its rippling mane the colour of the moon, its nostrils flared and its coat gleaming like starlight. On its back was a woman with fierce silver eyes and hair as dark as night. In her hand was a sword, and as she held it aloft her lips formed words that they couldn't hear, and her implacable gaze was firmly fixed on Guthrum alone.

He stood frozen for a moment, but the others had had enough. They were falling over themselves to get away, almost tumbling down the hillside in superstitious terror.

At last, as if in a dream, he moved – not away from her, but towards her, almost stumbling in his eagerness. But he was too late. The smoke from the strange fires had sunk lower, and it curled and crept and writhed along the ground as if it were a living creature that sought him out, and wrapped him in its smothering folds until he fell to the ground, clawing at the air as if he could tear the smoke away. He only vaguely heard the sound of not one, but two horses galloping off westwards along the ancient Wessex Ridgeway. And he certainly

226

didn't hear them trotting down into the valley a few miles further on, where a covered cart waited for them, and whoops of delighted glee signalled a task well done.

No one in Glastonbury expected to see the strangers again. They had followed close on the heels of the Danes, and what kind of madness was that? Oswyn's wife had told him he was a fool to let them take his best horses.

"You won't see them again," she told him crossly. "I don't know what you were thinking of, letting that Math talk you into it. You can never trust a Britisher, I've always said so and now you can see I'm right!"

And Oswyn had to admit, to himself if not to her, that she probably was.

But the next morning, there was a commotion out on the streets, and he heard the rhythmic clip-clop of horses' hooves and the rumble of a heavily laden cart. Cautiously, he peered out of the door, wondering nervously if the Danes had come back for more.

But it wasn't the Danes. Astonished, he saw his own horses, looking just as healthy as they had done the day before, if a bit tired. He tumbled into the street and stood staring after them. Math saw him and raised a hand.

"I told you we'd be back," he called. "Come to the abbey. Tell everyone to come!"

In ones and twos, the townspeople slipped out of their

houses, looking cautiously over their shoulders just in case the strangers had brought more trouble with them.

Apart from the blackened roof of the granary, the abbey looked remarkably peaceful, with only the rows of freshly dug graves in the monks' graveyard to show the recent slaughter.

Alfred turned his horse round to face the people and sat straight and tall in the saddle. Math was on one side of him, Oswald on the other. Cerys and Fleda stood beside the cart. People were shifting from one foot to the other, muttering and glancing curiously at it.

Alfred's steady gaze swept over all of them till they settled down. Then he began to speak.

"Yesterday, a terrible wrong was done here. Innocent blood was shed, as so much has been shed since the Northmen first came here. From north to south, from east to west, the Danes have plundered and destroyed, killed and maimed.

"Yesterday also, I heard one of you say that there was no one to care for you, no one to protect you. Well, that man was wrong. Because your king is here, and he will protect you!"

He drew his sword and pointed it up into the air. "I am Alfred, king of Wessex – and with God's will, I shall remain so! I will drive the Northmen out of our land, and I will make such a job of it that they will end by begging us for terms. This is the beginning, and you are here to see it!"

He leapt down from his horse and strode over to the cart. With his sword, he ripped away the sacking that covered the contents of the cart. Then, transferring the sword to his left hand, he grasped the reliquary of St Patrick in his right one and held it triumphantly aloft.

"As your abbot lay dying, I promised him that I would bring back this hallowed relic, which the abbey has treasured since long ago, when St Patrick himself walked here. The heathens stole it from the high altar. With his last breath, Herefyrth laid it on me that in retrieving it, I should not kill Guthrum."

He looked round at them slowly, his eyes fierce and determined. "I honoured his wish, and Guthrum lives. But I'm telling you this. Just as I've taken from Guthrum all that he gained from yesterday's raid, so when we meet again, I shall take from him all that he has left – including his life.

"There is food, too. Hide it and everything else too, in case Guthrum comes this way again. But there's nothing to lead him here: he'll be puzzling for many a long day over the robbers who dared to steal from the North-men!"

With his sword in one hand and the reliquary in the other, his face broke into a broad smile of triumph as they all burst into cheers. There was a buzz of excitement: the travellers were the centre of attention. Everyone wanted to get close to Alfred, to touch his cloak, to be assured that it was all true, that he really was the king.

When they began unloading the cart under Oswyn's direction, an elderly monk came over to speak to Alfred. He began to kneel, but Alfred stopped him with a gesture, and he smiled gratefully.

"I am sorry for your loss," said the king gently. "You must forgive me – I don't think we met yesterday. Or perhaps you weren't here?"

The monk looked puzzled for a moment, and then his face cleared.

"Oh, I see! No, no – I am not from Glastonbury. My name is Matthew, and I am the prior of Markham. I was travelling to the abbey yesterday, to speak with Herefyrth. I saw the smoke rising from a distance…" He shook his head, as if to rid it of sights he had no wish to remember. "By the time I arrived, the deed had been done. I could do nothing but help to bury the dead."

"Matthew." Alfred frowned. The name meant something: he knew he'd heard it recently. Then his face lightened. "Aethelnoth spoke to me of you! Of you and Guthrum. And how he didn't kill you."

Matthew smiled again and lifted his hands slightly. "As you see, God is good."

"But he wasn't to Herefyrth," pointed out Alfred.

Matthew looked at him, considering. "No. And yet Herefyrth asked you to spare Guthrum."

"Yes," said Alfred. "And I respected his wish. But I'll admit I don't understand it."

"Could you have killed him?"

Alfred thought. "No," he admitted. "No, not then. He was surrounded by his men. I was never close to him."

"But if you had been? Would you still have honoured Herefyrth's request?"

"I would have found it very difficult. But it was a promise to a dying man. It would have been one duty to set against another. I don't know," he said honestly. "I don't know what I would have done."

The monk's milky blue eyes looked at him steadily. "But you can see that there was a choice to be made. To kill, or to allow to live."

Alfred stared at him. "Perhaps. But now let me ask *you* something. What exactly happened between you and Guthrum? He killed Herefyrth. He's killed many other priests. Why did he spare you? He's not noted for his merciful qualities."

The blue eyes looked away from Alfred, seeming to focus on some imaginary distance beyond the walls of the church.

"Every man is a mixture," he said. "For each of us, there are many paths we can take. Some are obvious and easy; others are in shadow, and usually we don't even consider them. But sometimes the dark path happens to be lit by a fugitive ray of sunshine, and so that's the one we choose. That's what happened to Guthrum. He saw another path, and that day, for some reason, he was ready to take it."

Fleda found all this very difficult to follow, and she

could see that her father was puzzled too. Matthew apologized. "Forgive me. I'm not giving you a simple answer. But then it wasn't a simple question. How can I explain it better? When I looked at Guthrum, I saw somebody who was tired. Someone who was very alone. I think he saw himself reflected in my eyes, and it shocked him. That's all."

"You think he's tired?"

"Yes." Matthew paused. "But I'm a priest, not a soldier. I don't know how you're going to fight him. But if you win – and God willing, I think you will – think twice about what you should do next. What if you could not only save Wessex, but save Guthrum too?"

"What?" Alfred stared at him in astonishment.

"Guthrum and his people are pagans. They walk in darkness. Just think what a gift it would be for God – and for Herefyrth – if you could bring him into the Christian faith!"

Alfred was quiet for a moment. Then he said, "I will think about what you've said. But the first thing is to beat him in battle. Nothing matters more than that."

As they rode back to Athelney, Fleda thought about what the old priest had said. Forgiveness? It sounded all very fine. But if it turned out that Guthrum or any of his men had harmed her mother, or her brother and sisters, she knew that she would be more than happy to pick up a sword and kill him herself. She remembered Ulric's words of hatred about Guthrum when they had just arrived in Athelney; she remembered the terrible look in his eyes. She understood it now.

Easter: 878

OVER THE NEXT FEW WEEKS, Athelney became a hive of activity. Alfred and Aethelnoth sent messengers to every hall, calling on the thegns to fulfil their duty, and to every hundred court in the shire, asking them to send men as soon as they could be spared from the spring sowing. Sometimes Fleda herself went, and though the people were surprised to see a child speaking to them, and a girl at that, they listened when she spoke to them of her father's vision.

"There is this one last battle to fight," she told them seriously. "Guthrum is tired. Together, we can beat him. My father is fighting for all the people, and when he wins, he's going to make Wessex strong, and he's going to make it better for everyone. All you have to do is join him! We can do it together!"

Buds swelled and unfurled into leaves, and green shoots pushed exuberantly upwards through the warming soil, and hope grew. The king was alive! Stories spread of riders who appeared from no one knew where, to stage lightning attacks on Guthrum's camps and seize food and supplies: the raiders were being raided, and the hearts of the people lifted.

Ulric was kept busy helping Björn to fix old weapons and forge new ones. Alfred insisted that everyone was to be equipped with rectangular shields too, which must be just the same in size and shape, so that they would fit closely together. Talking to Fleda about Judith and Baldwin had reminded him of some of the lessons Baldwin had passed onto him from the court school.

"The Romans used to make a wall with their shields, and fight behind it," explained Alfred. "We can do that too. Then while the enemy waste time hurling themselves against our shields, our archers can fire above our heads and pick them off. They won't know what's hit them!"

Oswald had voiced what Ulric had been thinking. "That's fine as long as the archers know their job. What if the arrows fall short?"

"We'll train them. *You'll* train them. You and Erluin. You're good with the bow."

And the long, low green mound of Athelney became a training ground, from which the raiding parties went out to strike at the Northmen. The men of Somerset had the advantage: they knew the land, and could appear suddenly out of the mist and marshes, as if by magic.

Actually, they fought in the conventional way, not with sorcery or trickery, but the Danes were thrown off balance and became jittery and edgy.

Björn was a highly skilled craftsman, and Ulric threw himself into learning as much as he could from him. The smith was skilled at forging steel, which made a better cutting edge than iron, and under his tuition Ulric became expert at knowing the right moment to use the tongs to extract the billets of iron from the fire, manhandle them onto the anvil and hold them – just so – for Björn to weld them together with one blow. The timing had to be perfect or the metal would cool too much. Ulric learned to watch Björn's face closely, so that he could tell by the flicker of an eyelid when it was time to move. The work was hard, but Ulric enjoyed learning a new craft. His shoulders and arms ached at first, but soon they grew stronger.

Sometimes he was vaguely aware of Fleda watching him at work, and he wished he had time to stop and talk to her. But there was no time – he knew that what he was doing was important. All the same, sometimes he felt envious when he saw the fighting men ride out along the causeway, and he was quietly determined that at the end, when the whole army was gathered and ready to challenge Guthrum, he would be there. His fight with Guthrum was personal. He fully intended to weald weapons, as well as make them.

* * *

Fleda watched everything, determined to learn. People became used to her presence on the edge of things. But watching wasn't enough. Quietly, she began to join in when the men were training. She'd practised sword strokes with Edward, and learned what he'd learned from the armourer. She saw no reason why she shouldn't learn more. It was assumed that she was there with her father's blessing, and she saw no need to explain otherwise.

She asked Ulric to make a small sword for her. He looked doubtful, but she smiled and fixed him with her dark-fringed, blue-eyed gaze, and said surely he thought she should be able to defend herself, and somehow he found himself doing as she had asked. After all, it was a good practice piece for him to work on. Björn helped him, showing him how to sharpen the edge of the blade on the grindstone.

Cerys watched all this without comment, until one day she asked Fleda to go with her into the forest to hunt for plants that she needed for medicines. It was a relief to leave the confines of the island for a while. Trailing her hand in the water, Fleda looked back as the punt pulled away. It never failed to amaze her how quickly Athelney disappeared behind the trees and reed beds. Even now, with all the activity, no one would suspect its existence unless they actually stumbled on the causeway, and now there were enough men to ensure that only welcome visitors were allowed to get anywhere near East Lyng, where the causeway began.

Soon they were walking in the woods. Easter had passed, and rivers of bluebells flowed beneath the trees.

"You like to use a sword?" asked Cerys abruptly.

Fleda darted a glance at her. Cerys didn't miss much.

"It's good exercise," she said innocently.

"Would your mother be pleased if she knew you were learning swordplay alongside your father's soldiers?"

"She's not here," pointed out Fleda.

"I know that," said Cerys sharply. "And I think you're taking advantage of it. There will be a battle, and it will be terrible. More terrible than you can imagine … and yet I could almost think you were preparing yourself to take part in it, if it wasn't such a ridiculous idea."

Fleda examined her feet.

"Do you remember Uhtred?" said Cerys. "Do you remember Herefyrth?" Fleda shivered, and Cerys went on remorselessly. "This battle will be a thousand times worse. Fleda – I hope you aren't thinking for a minute that you can pretend to be a boy and fight in it. Even if you were a boy, you'd be much too young."

"I won't be left behind," said Fleda passionately. "I won't stay here and just wait." *Because what if it goes wrong? What if Father doesn't come back? What would I do then?*

Cerys looked at the bunch of leaves she had already collected.

"After the battle, there will be need of healing," she said. "You could help me. It's much more difficult to heal than it is to kill." She shrugged and turned away. "But

238

perhaps you couldn't do it. You're only a child, after all. There would be a great deal to learn. More than you could manage, I expect."

Fleda bristled and pulled a leaf from Cerys's hand. "What's that?" she demanded. "What does it do? How do you use it?"

The silver eyes flashed with secret amusement. "Why," said Cerys, "it's woundwort. It helps to stop bleeding. You crush the leaves, and you use them to make a poultice. See, like this…"

Egbert's Stone: May 878

I T WAS TIME. Over the weeks, messengers had ridden all over Wessex, carrying the same words: *Your king lives and has need of you. Prepare for battle, and when you receive word, be ready to ride.*

The word had been given. The time was seven weeks after Easter, and the king and the men of Somerset had ridden from the hidden fortress on Athelney to Egbert's Stone, an ancient meeting place on the side of a low hill where Wiltshire, Dorset and Somerset met. There they would wait for the men from the other shires.

Alfred and his men had climbed the hill together. Across the valley was a range of hills, a series of smooth curves almost bare of trees, dipping into valleys that had been hollowed out by water and wind, dapple-patterned by clouds racing across the sun. Down in the valley the River Deverill meandered through the flat grassland, widening out as it reached the village. Alfred had stopped there and prayed beside the wooden cross that stood by the bridge.

The men rested, sitting on the sheep-nibbled turf in the spring sunshine as they waited. But the king went up onto the mound of flint and earth that was named Egbert's Stone, and sat alone there, thinking.

Soon they will come, the men of Wiltshire and Hampshire and Somerset. They will march along the valley and up the hill, and I will stand above them on this mound, and I'll begin to speak. And I'll know from their faces whether all we've done, all I've said, has been enough. Enough to make them believe that we can win. Because if they believe it, we will. This is our time.

Here it is peaceful, and yet our business is war. Behind me, the wind sighs in the trees. It sounds like the sea, constantly crashing onto the shore, trickling away, then gathering itself for another onslaught. Relentless, wild. Lonely.

Opposite is King's Hill. It's called that because of my grandfather, Egbert, who came here after another battle – over the British of Cornwall that time. So many battles, so much blood lost…

How many will come? Will there be enough?

Suddenly rooks scattered from the shelter of the trees, calling in raucous alarm. They spiralled up like smoke against the sky, and then reeled back down again to roost. Far down in the valley, sun glinted on metal. Fleda strained to see. There were men, some on foot and some on horseback, emerging from the narrowest part of the valley, heading up the hill towards them. Men and more men, and then more again – a river, a torrent of soldiers! Her father was standing up on top of the mound,

241

outlined against the sky, his cloak blowing in the wind, the sunlight flashing on the gold circlet he wore. His stern face broke into the broadest of smiles, and he drew his sword and waved it in the air. A cheer broke out. It was ragged at first, then more and more voices took it up till it became a roar of welcome, echoing across the valley.

"It's like something in a story!" said Fleda.

"Yes," said Cerys. "I think he knows that. He couldn't have chosen a better place to meet them. Look at their faces! You'd think he'd risen from the dead!"

But Fleda could hardly hear her above the noise. The enthusiasm was catching, and she found herself laughing in delight.

Some time later, thousands of men were gathered at the foot of the mound. There were so many that hardly a blade of grass could be seen. Alfred raised his hands, and gradually they all fell silent.

"This is the best of days!" he said, grinning round at them. "See how many we are? See how mighty we are? Does Guthrum stand a chance? Does he? Of course he doesn't! Wessex will be ours again!"

More cheering, and more.

Then he said, "You are my welcome guests. And as my guests, I have prepared a feast for you." He reached down and brandished a loaf of bread in each hand. "I made this! Yes, me! Well – I got it out of the oven anyway." Laughter. Someone at the front called something out, and he grinned. "All right, it may be a little burnt. Just a very little. But my point is, you have come here, away from your homes and families, to fight. For yourselves, but at my bidding. I owe you a debt for this. And I will repay it. After this battle I will build you a better country. A stronger country, where we don't have to scuttle away in fear when the Danes come knocking. "A country…" he paused, and looked round at them. "A country that will stretch beyond the borders of Wessex. A country for all the English-speaking peoples! We'll have such a peace that no one will need to choose between fighting and growing crops." He was serious now, as he looked slowly round at them all. "This I promise you."

He paused, and in the silence there was nothing to be heard but the sighing of the wind in the trees. Then he went on. "Tonight we will camp here, and tomorrow at Iley Oak, further up the river. Guthrum's camp is at Edington. The day after tomorrow, we will march over Battlesbury Hill to meet him. And we will win. We are fresh and he is tired. This is our country, and we will win it back!"

He looked round them, his eyes calm and tranquil. Then he grinned. "So lose the long faces! The bread may be burnt but, so help me, it's fresh! Let's break it together, and share songs and stories, for tonight at least!" He waved the loaf about as if it were a sword, and his laughter infected the men, and they cheered loudly.

243

Then they made camp, and later on the night was lit by the glow of many fires, and Alfred visited each of them, so that every man felt he had been singled out, and all of them felt certain of success.

The Eve of the Battle

SILENCE HUNG OVER THE CAMP. It was the last night before the battle, and although thousands of men were camped close together within the sheltering loop of the River Wyle, each of them felt as if he was alone, with only his own thoughts to comfort or disturb him.

Ulric lay on his back, gazing up towards the ridge. Somewhere on the other side of it was Guthrum. Did he know how close they were? Did he feel afraid? Ulric hoped so, though he knew it wasn't likely. You had to have imagination to be afraid, and someone who could kill like Guthrum surely couldn't have any imagination, or he'd never sleep at night.

It was a clear night and a cold one, even though it was late spring now. All he could see of the ridge was a black shape against the night sky, like a brooding, sleeping animal.

He supposed that everyone else was asleep. It was very quiet, very still – not like last night. Then, people had been singing songs and telling stories and laughing, bragging about other battles they'd fought in. Ulric had joined in the laughter and enjoyed the companionship, but he had no stories of his own; this would be his first battle.

He'd always thought his father would be there beside him for the first time, that he would talk to him quietly, telling him what to expect, what it was going to be like. The words wouldn't really matter – it would be enough just to hear his father's voice, deep and steady, and to be at his side.

But thanks to Guthrum, he wasn't there. He wasn't anywhere. He wasn't even properly buried – Ulric hated to think of that. The familiar thoughts began to churn through his mind – he should have waited, he should have done something.

But that was then, and this was now. Ulric tried to make himself breathe slowly and regularly. He was frightened. He could admit it to himself, though not to anyone else here. He was scared of being scared tomorrow, scared he'd be useless, that he'd shame himself. But there was one thing he knew for sure. If he got the chance, he'd kill Guthrum. He didn't care how, he wasn't going to be honourable about it. Guthrum didn't deserve honour. Ulric would do whatever he had to do – he'd stab him from behind, or throw rocks at him, or stick the point of his sword in his eyes. If he got the chance, which he knew he probably wouldn't.

At the very least, he hoped for the chance to watch Guthrum die. Really, really slowly. Perhaps from a stomach wound. They were said to be the worst.

Oswald always found it hard to sleep before a battle. Usually he would just sit quietly, thinking a little bit. He was ready, all prepared. Sword, knife and axe – they were as sharp as Björn could make them, ready to taste Danish flesh. When he drew his sword through the air, it sang a deadly song: singing for blood, singing for victory.

For a while, back there in the marshes, he had thought it wasn't going to come right. He'd never seen Alfred like that before. It was a hard thing for all of them, running away from Chippenham, running for cover. Oh, he knew it was what they'd had to do – his head could see the sense of it. But not his heart. That told him they should have made a stand and fought, even if there'd been no hope at all. Yes, yes, he knew they would have died – but what a brave and honourable end it would have been!

He'd wondered if Alfred was ever going to recover in those dark days on Athelney. But he had. Whether it was Cerys and her potions, or the presence of Fleda, or the will of God, or his own strong heart, Oswald didn't know. But here he was, and here they were, all of them. And tomorrow they were going to win. They'd go up over Battlesbury Hill, and they'd fall on the Northmen like a hawk on a mouse. He'd never felt this sure, the night before a battle. Yesterday, at Egbert's Stone – how all the men had cheered when they'd seen the king! It was almost as if they'd thought he'd come back from the dead. Though come to think of it, in a way he had...

Cerys watched the moon, pale and silver, almost full, soon to be a thin crescent again. Everything changes, she mused. The moon grows, and then she wanes, and then she grows again. The tides rise, and fall back, and rise again. The trees come into bud, then into leaf, and when winter comes, the branches are bare again. Everything has its place, everything has its time.

And this, now, was to be Alfred's time. She felt sure of it. As the year had grown strong, so had he. He would win the battle. She was sure of it, and then he would begin to rebuild.

But first, there had to be the killing. How many of these men would tomorrow lie shattered on the field of battle, carrion for crows?

Was there no other way?

There wasn't, she knew. She sighed, and slipped like a shadow into the woods to gather some herbs she'd noticed earlier. They were more powerful when picked by the light of the moon.

Fleda lay as still as she could, her eyes squeezed shut. She knew she needed to go to sleep, but the thoughts kept jumping about in her head, and she couldn't. It would be the closest she had ever come to a battle, and she was frightened, but she was excited too. Cerys had said it would be terrible, and she understood what she meant – but it wouldn't be like the massacre at Glastonbury. That had been brutal, a blasphemy.

But this would be different, wouldn't it? You only had to look round at all these brave men who'd come to fight for her father; you only had to remember their joy when they'd seen him yesterday. No one could stand against them, no one. They were heroes, all of them. People would sing songs about them one day, like the songs she'd heard last night.

But some of them would be dead by this time tomorrow.

Not Oswald, strong, kindly Oswald, she thought uneasily. Not Erluin, quick tempered but eager and brave. Nor Ricbert, with his cheerful face and sharp eyes, or Eadric, who loved to make jokes. And especially not Ulric. He'd suffered enough already. And her father wasn't allowed to die – that went without saying.

She began to pray. For all of them.

She fell asleep wondering if she would soon be seeing her mother and Edward again. It was better to think about that. Better to think good thoughts...

Alfred pulled the blanket up closer round his daughter's shoulders. A little night breeze ruffled her hair, and he stroked her cheek gently. She shouldn't be here. He should have left her safe in Athelney. But if the unthinkable happened – if they lost – she wouldn't be safe anywhere. Cerys had promised to keep her well away from the battle, and he trusted Cerys, even though she mystified him.

He found a tree to lean against, wanting to be alone. He would sleep for a few hours a little later, but at the moment he still felt wide awake. His senses were alert and on guard: he could smell the fresh scent of the soil, the faint scent of bluebells and the sharp tang of fox in the woods that covered the lower part of the hill near the river. He could hear faint rustlings among the leaves, and the low hoot of an owl hunting. He could see the deep, rich blue of the evening sky, scattered with brilliant stars, and he wondered if Guthrum was looking at it too. Probably not: he would be comfortably tucked up in Alfred's manor in Edington, below the white horse where they'd tricked Guthrum and won back the Glastonbury treasure.

Had that been the start of the way back, he wondered? It was certainly at that point that word had begun to spread, that hope had begun to grow.

But the real turning point had been earlier, when he'd begun to recover from his illness. It had been a new start; he really had felt as if he'd been born again, as if everything was fresh to him. As he'd listened to each person – to Cerys and Math and Oswald and Erluin and Ulric, and later to Björn and Aethelnoth and Herefyrth and Matthew, and as he'd talked to Fleda, remembering the past and learning lessons from it – he'd taken something from all of them.

And now he knew what he was going to do. He was going to defeat Guthrum and save Wessex. Maybe, just maybe, he would save Guthrum too. And then it would be time to make a success of the peace.

The Battle of Edington

GUTHRUM SNAPPED AWAKE IRRITABLY. That dratted dream again! He was blundering round in a thick fog, and every instinct he possessed told him that Alfred was close – very close. He stood still, and slowly moved his great head from side to side, listening and gazing, trying to pierce the mist with his eagle eyes.

But try as he might, he couldn't find him, and then, just as he let out a terrific bellow of rage, he heard mocking laughter, great whoops of it, echoing all round his head, inside and outside.

That was the dream. And then he would wake up. Witchcraft, that was what it was. That silver-eyed horsewoman was at the back of it, he knew it. Since her appearance, everything had gone wrong. Alfred had suddenly and unaccountably sprung to life again, and instead of being the hunters, Guthrum's men had become the hunted, which was very uncomfortable and embarrassing. They'd been stolen from, laughed at and made fools of. And now, Alfred was even stealing sleep from him!

Furious, he lay down again. There was a nagging ache in one of his teeth, and he lay on that cheek to try and deaden the pain. That *was probably witchcraft as well…*

"Sire! Sire!"

Groaning, Guthrum sat up. Who dared to wake him? Did these people have no sense of self-preservation? He would make it his personal mission to ensure that someone would suffer for this.

"Ivar?" he said in disbelief. Surely he should know better.

"The ridge, my lord! Up on the ridge," stammered Ivar.

"What? What are you talking about? What's up on the ridge?"

"I – I think you'd better come and see, my lord…"

Cursing his stiff back, Guthrum lumbered outside. Dawn had broken. He looked blearily up at the ridge that lowered over Edington, dark and foreboding. Suddenly sharply awake, he stared. There was something very wrong with the clean line the ridge normally etched against the sky. It was the wrong shape: it bristled. And there was the glint of metal…

"In Odin's name," whispered Guthrum, "how can this be? WHERE HAVE THEY COME FROM?"

There was no answer: just an appalled silence from the men behind him, as they stared up at the army that had so unexpectedly amassed up above.

The men of Wessex stood in a line just below the top of the ridge. Their shields fitted together to form a formidable, impenetrable wall, just as Alfred had intended.

Alfred stood in the centre of the line. He felt astonishingly calm as he looked down on the Danes, who were milling about at the bottom of the hill in confusion. By the time they had sorted themselves out and cobbled together a charge that would bring them to the top, they would be out of breath and exhausted. And in that moment, the archers would let loose their deadly rainfall of arrows to bring fear and chaos to an already wrong-footed army.

The air up here on the ridge was sweet and cool. Alfred breathed it in deeply, and lifted his eyes from the scurrying Northmen to gaze beyond them at the vast Wiltshire plain which stretched as far as the lilac blue line where land met sky. Beyond that, he knew, was Mercia, reaching hundreds of miles to the north. By the end of today, he promised himself, Wessex would be free of the threat of Danish rule. After that, perhaps Mercia – and then, why not the rest of the English-speaking kingdoms? He could bring them together as one great state!

Here came the enemy, a disorganized but still formidable army, charging, stumbling up the steep slope.

Slowly, Alfred raised his arm. It was almost time.

The sounds of battle battered the ears: men shouted, screamed, grunted in pain; horses whinnied and neighed in shrill terror; the ugly clash of metal on metal. And the smell: that overwhelming stench of blood, sweat, fear and fury, all encompassing.

Through it all, Alfred searched for Guthrum. The Danish chief had been at the centre of the mass of men as they swarmed up the hill, impossible to miss: a big man with flying yellow hair, half a head taller than anyone else, his features distorted by a prolonged yell of fury. Then came the arrows, and as the Danes reeled under the onslaught Alfred gave the command, and the Saxons broke their shield wall to ram home their advantage. After that it was impossible to see anything but the particular enemy in front of him, to do anything but wield his great sword in a series of efficient twists and jabs, to answer the needs of the moment. Till at last there came a time when he paused for breath and caught sight of the giant with yellow hair not ten yards away.

Guthrum's hands were raised, clutching his sword, about to drive it down into a body already lying on the ground. But there was another figure slightly behind and to one side, someone Guthrum hadn't seen. It was Ulric, and Alfred could see what he was doing; he had placed himself in such a way that while Guthrum's attention was on the other man, Ulric would be able to drive his knife into Guthrum's side.

Time seemed to have slowed into a series of pictures. Alfred knew what would happen next: Guthrum would twist round as he was struck, and take Ulric down with him.

Alfred roared out Guthrum's name. The Danish chief saw him, and bared his teeth in a savage grin of acknowledgement. In the same second, he noticed Ulric, and swatted him away as if he was a fly.

But then someone crashed into Alfred, knocking him

to the ground. The man had been killed by a sword thrust, and by the time Alfred had managed to roll the body off him and stagger to his feet, the tide of the battle had carried Guthrum in a different direction. Their meeting would have to wait.

Fleda was beside herself with frustration. She and Cerys were waiting along the ridge to the west of Edington in the shelter of a belt of trees; they had only a limited view of what was happening. Math had promised to do his best to keep them informed, but he had warned them that it would be difficult; he wouldn't be able to leave the battle unless it was very clearly going their way. Restlessly, she turned to Cerys.

"Can't you do anything?" she pleaded. "Couldn't you wrap us in mist, or something, so we could get closer?"

"Mist doesn't stop a sword or an axe," said Cerys shortly. "You'll just have to be patient."

"Oh! There are the arrows! See? Just as Father planned. And…" Fleda fell silent, her forehead creased in concentration. At a distance, it was impossible to tell who was on which side. It was a confused turmoil, with hundreds of desperate fights taking place everywhere, and to her horrified eyes it seemed that everyone was equally savage: Danes and Saxons alike fought without mercy.

Cerys put her arm round the girl's shoulders, but Fleda pulled away, her face pale but determined. "No. I must watch. This is how it is, isn't it? I have to see, even if I can't fight."

It soon became clear that the Saxons were pushing the Danes, slowly but inexorably, down the hill. Taken by surprise, exhausted by the rush uphill and then decimated by the onslaught of arrows, the Danes were giving way, retreating down the hill, then fleeing north across the plain. Long before Math came to tell them, Cerys and Fleda could see it was over. He had brought a horse for them.

"For you," he gasped. "They're on the run, heading towards Chippenham. We're going to follow them, mop up the stragglers. The king says for you to use the manor at Edington to treat the wounded. They're being carried down already, and there will be people to help you."

It was chaos at first, but eventually under Cerys's direction the wounded were sorted out into those who were only slightly hurt, those with more serious injuries and those for whom death was only a matter of time. Cerys pushed Fleda firmly towards the first group, and Fleda was secretly thankful. She'd glimpsed some of the worst wounds: one man had a bloody stump where his arm should be; another was staring down at his stomach in bewilderment, trying to hold it. The stench and the cries of pain were more than she could cope with, and she felt numb with horror as she went into the barn where the less seriously injured men were. She had not yet seen anyone she knew: there was at least that to be thankful for.

Then she saw a familiar face. It was Ulric. With a cry, she hurried over to him, almost stumbling in her eagerness. He had no visible wound, but he was lying very still. His face was pale and his eyes were closed. She knelt beside him.

"Don't be dead, Ulric!" she whispered. "Oh, please don't be dead!" She touched his cheek. It was warm, he was breathing and she closed her eyes and muttered a short prayer of thanks. What should she do? Clumsily, she felt his head. Something felt sticky, and when she looked at her fingers there was a little blood on them. As gently as she could, she explored further, till she found a bump on the back of his skull.

She sat back and looked at him.

"You're not going to die," she said firmly. "I won't have it!"

For hour after hour, Ulric lay still, his face as pale and still as marble. But not as cold. He still lived. Whenever she could, Fleda left her other patients to sit beside him. If she talked to him – if only she could find the right words – somehow she would be able to draw him back from wherever he was.

She talked to him about Athelney, about the marshes and the lakes and the piercing, lonely cries of the water birds. She spoke of the bitter blizzard they'd travelled through when they first came there, and told him what a good cook he was, and how much he'd helped when her father had been ill. She told him that all his friends needed him: Oswald, Ricbert, Erluin, Eadric, Cerys, Math, Fleda herself and her father, the king. She whispered into his ear that he must get better, because now that her father was going to regain his kingdom, there would be much to do, and Ulric had to be part of that.

And finally, on the second day, she sensed that there was a change. There was some colour in his cheeks, and there were tiny movements, almost imperceptible, in the muscles of his face.

"He's waking up! Look, his eyelids are twitching!" Fleda was beside herself with excitement, and Cerys hurried over.

"Ulric?" said Cerys gently.

His eyes slowly opened. He looked at Cerys, and then at Fleda. He smiled, but it looked painful, and Fleda reached for a cup of water. She had moistened his lips with water all the time he had been unconscious, but still, he would be very thirsty. She and Cerys helped him to sit up, in the way Cerys had shown her, and then she helped him to sip from the cup.

At last he was able to speak.

"I'm alive," he said. "I dreamed I was dead."

Cerys smiled back at him. "You weren't allowed to die. The princess said so. And she sat and watched you to make sure of it."

Fleda blushed. "It wasn't such a bad wound, that's all. You were just unconscious for a while. Nearly two days, in fact. Can you remember what happened?"

He frowned. "I saw Guthrum. I was very close, and I was going to kill him. But then – I don't know what came next. What's happening now? Did we win?"

"Yes. Guthrum fled," said Cerys. "He's under siege in Chippenham with what's left of his army. But he won't last long. He'll have to give in soon."

Ulric closed his eyes again for a moment. When he opened them, they were as clear and fresh as a summer sky.

"I hated him so much," he said quietly. "Death was all I could think about. But now, life seems more important."

Late May, 878

GUTHRUM STOOD BEFORE ALFRED. The siege was over, and the Danes had surrendered. Guthrum's hands were bound behind his back. He looked gaunt and exhausted, but the sea-coloured eyes beneath the shaggy brows were still defiant.

"So," he growled. "Face to face again. How are you, Alfred?"

Alfred grinned mirthlessly. "Better than you," he replied.

Guthrum nodded wearily. "Get on with it then," he said. "What's it to be? Arrows? Sword thrust? Hanging? Or is there some special way you do it in Wessex? Come on, Alfred, what's your fancy?"

"None of those," said Alfred. He signalled to one of his men. "Untie him." Then he folded his arms and smiled.

"You and I," he said, "are going to talk."

* * *

Ulric and Fleda stood before Alfred. He had sent for them, and after the informality of life in Athelney, it felt strange to follow the king's messenger into the great hall. Alfred was sitting in his tall oak chair, and he indicated that they were to sit opposite him. Also round the table were Oswald, Cerys, Eadric, Ricbert, Math and Erluin. The king looked round at all of them before he began to speak. He sat very straight, and his eyes were sparkling with warmth and energy.

"There is a special bond between those of us who were in Athelney," he said. "Soon, I will announce to the world what I have decided. But first, I want to explain it to you." His eyes rested fleetingly on Ulric.

"Guthrum and his chiefs are going to become Christians; I myself will stand as godfather. I think he feels that our God has proved to be stronger than his … or maybe he's just had enough of being forever on the move. Whatever the reason, he has taken a step towards a new life. He will withdraw to the east, beyond a line which we have agreed, called the Danelaw, and there he will stay – or pay the price. If he breaks the agreement this time, the next time there will be no mercy, and he knows that. But if the peace holds – and I think it will – it will be a great victory for God.

"And so now we have time. Time to rebuild, time to make Wessex strong again. And after that, who knows? Perhaps one day all the kingdoms of this land will be as one."

Then he looked at Fleda, and his face relaxed into a huge smile.

"There are some people here whom I think you will be very glad to see!"

And he turned towards the door.

Following his glance, Fleda caught her breath, hardly able to believe what was happening. A number of people, small and large, were tumbling through the door, laughing and eager. First was Edward, rushing up to her and grabbing her hands. Then Aethelgifu and Aethelfrith, wrapping their arms round her legs. And finally, her mother, with a smile trembling through tears.

Then the king was with them. He flung his arms open, ready to enfold his family and keep them safe, together at last.

Cerys turned away, smiling but a little sad. And then Oswald, shy and nervous, touched her on the sleeve. He had something to ask, and he hoped she would consider it...

Wedmore: June 878

GUTHRUM AND HIS DANES LEFT YESTERDAY. For a time, at least, it's over. There is peace.

I breathe in the sweet smell of the hillside. Before me, a silver morning mist lies over the vale of Wedmore like a calm sea. The curved tops of trees float like shadowy blue clouds, and the small, isolated hills rise up like the islands they actually become when the rivers flood. The furthest one stands above the abbey at Glastonbury. It's a marker for this part of Wessex. Wherever you go, you see it, like a finger pointing to Heaven. It was there at Athelney, in the dark time. Sometimes it seemed like a beacon; sometimes more like a reproach.

But the true light of those days is here with me now — my daughter Fleda. She throws stones for the dogs, and her head goes back as her laughter sings out. The silver gilt sun catches on her hair where the tendrils spring loose, so she is framed with light. Soon, she will come and sit beside me on this rock, and she will ask me, a little shyly, what I am thinking.

And perhaps I will tell her. Perhaps I will say, yes, we have won this great battle. But that is only the beginning. Because now, we have to rebuild. Where the fields were laid waste, we must replant them. Where villages were destroyed, we must rebuild them. Where churches were plundered, and books were burned so that their words blew as ash into the air — we will build monasteries and nurture learning.

We nearly lost the world. Now we must make it safe, and make it better.

But perhaps I will say none of these things to her. Perhaps, for a little while longer, I will keep them locked away in my heart. For now, for this little space in time, she can be just a child, and I can be just a father. And then, we will go down the hill to my hall, and I will be the king again.

Author's Note

The peace of Wedmore did hold. Guthrum retreated behind an agreed line, into what became known as the Danelaw. Perhaps surprisingly, he held to the Christian faith, and he didn't fight Alfred again. Other Northmen did, but by then, Alfred had ordered fortified towns to be constructed, so that no one would be more than twenty miles from one, and in times of trouble the people could take shelter inside them. He also developed a new system of ensuring that there would not only be enough men to fight, but also enough to care for the land. It was quite simple: the men were divided into two groups, called fyrds, one of which was always on fighting duty and the other on farming duty.

Alfred respected the rights of the witangemot – the council of wise men – and accepted their help with governing the country. He wrote down the laws of the land. Perhaps as a result of his early travels, he reached out beyond the shores of Britain, sending missions to Rome and India, and corresponding with the Patriarch of Jerusalem. The Welsh or British, as they were called, then became his allies.

He realized it would make sense to have fighting ships ready to defend Wessex at sea, and is credited as the founder of the Royal Navy.

Alfred also established a court school, similar to Charlemagne's, inviting scholars from all over Europe to come and be part of it. He insisted that children be taught to read English, and he learned Latin so that he could translate great classical books into English. He commissioned the writing of the *Anglo-Saxon Chronicle*, a record of national events, which was to be kept for many years to come.

As for Fleda, she eventually became the lady of the Mercians, and was a formidable and very successful leader in her own right. But that's another story...

ACKNOWLEDGEMENTS

I would like to thank my agent, Lindsey Fraser, for her unfailing enthusiasm and encouragement, and my editor, Mara Bergman, for her patience and carefulness.

Thanks also to my sister, Maggie Barton, and my nieces, Sarah and Hannah, for all their interest and support during the writing of the story of Alfred. Hannah started studying Anglo Saxon history at university at about the same time I began writing the book, so it was lovely to compare notes as we both learnt more.

The staff of Glastonbury Abbey and Somerset Libraries were kind enough to share their expertise when I asked them such questions as whether Anglo Saxon churches had windows, or the whereabouts of Egbert's Stone, and for this I thank them, too.

When his younger sister Sophie has a stroke, twelve-year-old Tom feels jealous and guilty, impatient and scared all at the same time. His mate Ash is the only one that seems to understand. But Ash has problems of his own. His Dad has unexpectedly returned after years in and out of jail, and the fragile balance of Ash's family crumbles. But Sophie believes that the willow man is magical and can help them all: her to walk, Ash to read... But the willow man is burnt to the ground, taking with it all her dreams. Only by helping each other can the children mend their fractured lives.

Visit Sue at www.suepurkiss.com